CAN YOU TRUST
AN ALIEN?

Book One of the Trust Series

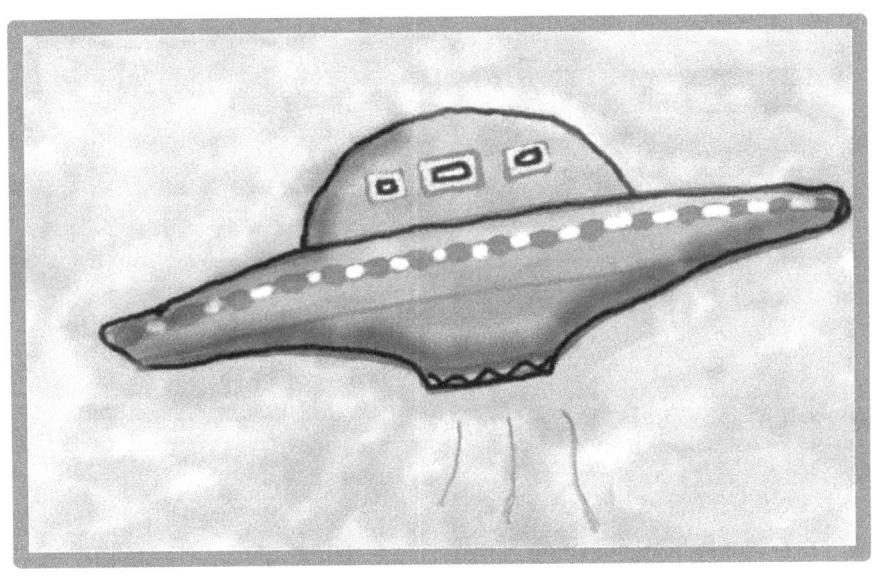

K.S. Riggin

Table of Contents

Chapter One: Prologue

I was used to making contact with aliens. When you work on the Exchange, that's your job. The system automatically translates alien tongues from all known galaxies, so Transtel-programmers can schedule arrivals, departures, and appointments for visiting ambassadors. Transtel-programming is an interesting job, and I enjoyed communicating with beings whose thought processes were different than Terrans'.

Isn't it strange that for every positive statement, there is a "but"? I know you're waiting for it. The "but" in my case was a Natharan named Captain Cegan. He's the reason why I no longer work at N.Y. Transtel Systems.

The first time he contacted me, the captain was still out in Bootes, the constellation of the Bear Watcher. My transprompter reported he was a Natharan, a species I'd never heard of. That "unknown species" part was kind of interesting, and I remember being curious about it, but our transystem was heavy that day. We were short on personnel because of an earlier mix-up with the flu vaccines, and I hadn't had much time to think about anything except keeping the transystem from jamming with too many "on hold" calls. Thankfully, the Natharan's computer carried all his ship's specs, so it was simple to chart the captain's course to Earth without any problem. If the captain stayed on schedule, he'd reach Earth in thirty-seven days.

I always carried about eighty ships in my transystem, with direct communication to each captain. (Earth policy demanded that all transystem communications be addressed by the ship's captain.) The Natharan's communication was normal. I scarcely would have remembered the contact if not for the captain's voice. His ship had an Enhancer. They weren't uncommon then, but out of all those ships on

1

the transystem that day, maybe only one or two carried them. The Enhancer allowed me to hear the captain's voice directly, translated, of course, but with his precise vocality (tone, cadence, pitch, and word usage). And, because of it, the Natharan was able to hear my voice, with my exact vocality.

So, I'll admit, even though I was too busy to give the captain my full concentration because of the heavy sequence of lights flashing on my transystem (often, a warning that backlogs were imminent), my memory of the captain's first call was still entirely too vivid to forget. Those shivers in my spine at hearing his luscious, deep baritone giving me his name, number, destination, and purpose — how could any female forget shivers like that?

And then, the next day, there'd been another transmission from him, not the usual protocol. If I'd been a different person, I suppose I would have protested or reported the captain's obstruction of my time. But I didn't. The truth is that, even then, I found the strange Natharan charming, and I suppose, therein lies the story.

Chapter Two: Definition of Alien,
A Foreigner

"Cegan from Natharan. Come in, please, Terra #5732698," he began that second contact.

"This is Terra #5732698, for Captain Cegan. Is there a problem or change in the program?" I asked.

"No change, no problem," he responded. Then he paused, and I heard him hum as if he were thinking, hesitating. His hum was musical, almost unchanging in its tone. It was somehow pleasing to hear. It made me want to wait, holding onto that note, as if in expectation of hearing a strange but longed for melody.

When Captain Cegan spoke again, it was as if I were released, free to turn away, to go on about my work — yet, the sound of his voice still invited me to listen.

"Your voice is feminine. Is this correct?" he asked.

I shook my head suddenly as if the movement were needed to separate me from the pull of the alien's voice. I cleared my throat and shakily got back to business. "Acknowledged," I said. "No change, no problem."

I paused and swallowed a second, wondering if I should address his question. Was it allowed? Was there any harm in answering him? Who would know?

I smiled. "Affirmative. I am female," I added, feeling a daring wildness that I normally lacked.

His ship must have had a sonar-augmenter. His voice replied to my words much faster than I expected.

3

"And your age?" he asked. "Are you married or spoken for? What color is your hair?"

I laughed before I flipped the transline back on to speak. Who wouldn't have, after months of hearing military formality and then hearing the party scene coming over my transystem? How could the captain mimic humans so well? Why did he want to?

Whatever his reasons, I was intrigued. "Eighteen years old," I answered him. "I don't have a husband or a boyfriend. My hair is auburn-brown."

I put my feet up on the desk and rationalized that it was really break time anyway. Who could object if I spent my time talking with some weirdo in space?

Once more, the captain hummed his note. "I am gratified to hear your marital status," he told me. Then his words came without pause as if he were afraid we'd be cut off. "You are very young. What is the average age of marriage on your planet? What is auburn? What is your name?"

I covered the mike and giggled at the silliness of what I was doing, but I found myself answering him. "I don't know the average age." I thought a moment and then guessed, "25?" I hadn't flipped the switch off. It was still my turn to talk, but I half-expected the alien captain to comment. Somehow, I could feel his impatience, or did I imagine it?

I paused to remember what he'd asked me. About my hair? He wanted to know what "auburn" meant. "Like autumn leaves, kind of reddish. My father calls it melted pennies, but I guess that doesn't mean anything to you. Pennies are our coins. They're made from copper."

I was babbling. I felt stupid. I started to flip the speaker button off, but I remembered his last question. "My name is Kira," I told the captain.

I straightened up, pulling my feet back down to the floor. My eyes checked the wall clock. The minute hand, a lime green caterpillar, edged sideways and down. I had five more minutes before my break was ended. I counted slowly, waiting for the response time: one, two, three . . .

"A pretty name," the captain shot back at me with that gorgeous baritone. When someone had a voice like that, it was hard to keep in mind that he was an alien. I shivered like a thirteen- year-old listening to a new sonic rhythm.

"I look forward to seeing your hair," he continued. "Is your hair long or short, Kira? What language do you speak?"

What a way to break up the monotony of a normal day. . . flirtation with an alien. I laughed at myself for playing such a silly game. I could be with my friends, chewing on a pretzel, sipping a cola . . . but, instead, I continued to play. "My hair falls down to the middle of my back. I speak Engspan," I told the captain. "Do you speak it?"

An expletive issued from the alien's mouth. The computer translated it as "darn." I wondered what kind of swear words were current on Natharan. Had I said the wrong thing? The company kept warning us in their bulletins how easy it was to insult one who didn't share your customs. Had I offended the captain? Would I get in trouble?

"I must go now," the Natharan said abruptly before I had a chance to apologize. "I have a minor problem here. I must learn your Engspan, Kira. I am not comfortable with a translator between us."

The click at the end of the transmit came immediately after. I was left staring at the light, the apology I'd wanted to offer unspoken.

Another call came in almost immediately. It was a Pethorian, zoning through our system. After that, there was a steady traffic of bookings and an assortment of problems, nothing out of the ordinary, just busy work that kept me occupied.

It was hours later before I had a chance to think about the Natharan and his sexy, velvety voice. Yet, when I did, when I finally had the chance to remember the things he'd said and the way he'd said them, I decided that it was more than the vocality of the captain's voice that stayed with me. I liked him. I liked the way the captain spoke. I smiled, remembering the "I am gratified to hear your marital status." Sure, it was the transystem translating, but it was the captain's style. He'd asked me for exactly what he wanted to know without hedging. I liked his candor and the way he promised to learn my language. I wished that New York men were more like the Natharan.

For the rest of the day, when I wasn't busy, I continued thinking about the alien. Had I made him angry? Would he report me? I didn't think he could, not unless he wanted to get himself in trouble for taking up transystem time. But had I said something wrong? What could have upset him? Would he call again?

It was crazy. I should never have engaged in conversation, not that kind anyway. Talking with aliens was far too risky. They were different from us, strange and weird looking. Yet, I'd had a good time talking with the Natharan. What was wrong with that?

When I arrived home that night and found myself still pondering over the alien captain's conversation, shivering delightedly over the humming and the gentle sweetness of his voice, I had to laugh. Sure, I liked his style and talking with him had been amusing, but aliens were my job, not my choice for dates.

Deliberately, I pushed him out of my mind and began to read one of the new best sellers by Seren Davec. It was her latest interactive and was supposed to be great fun. A friend had lent it to me and wanted it back the next day. I hooked in right after dinner, and for hours, my muscles twitched as I sat on the couch, solving a mystery in a delightfully nerve-wracking haunted house. By the time I'd finished and crawled into bed, my body and mind were exhausted. I collapsed under the sheets, pulled up the covers, and glanced over at the wall clock. I could have kicked myself. It was after three A.M.

I woke up the next morning with the cold-water spray of my alarm clock. It drenched me twice before I could pry my eyes open. I rose up, stretching and yawning, drained of energy and red-eyed from lack of sleep. My body ached. I was stiff as if I'd been the one chased up and down the stairs of the novel's creepy house. It took two cups of double caff for me to get back to even thinking about being pleasant to the world.

Once I got to the office, my body finally started to rev up. I was doing fine until I had a very rude and difficult Sarsquasian come onto my transline. He wanted to talk with the President of North America, and I kept explaining to the Sarsquasian that there was no such person or position. The alien called me a liar and swore at me with words that were translated as "languid biped" and "unwise female insect." Not even double caff could keep my head from pounding after that. I finally transferred the jerk to my boss, Mr. Dee.

Five minutes later, time enough for me to have swallowed two tran-laxer pills, my boss called me back. He'd not only fixed the problem, but he complimented my handling of the situation! That's what I call a great boss!

I was still floating in Mr. Dee's praise when the Natharan called again.

"Kira," he said, with a voice as smooth as vanilla mocha. I stared at the light on my transystem. Why hadn't the transline notified me of a caller? Had I missed the tell-tale bleep?

Hearing the captain's voice was so unexpected; it stunned me. It made me dizzy and confused. I clutched at my desk, needing the touch of it, the solidness of its fake wood stability. I couldn't speak.

"Kira," the captain said again. "Tell me I have not frightened you."

I was trembling, but I wasn't frightened. Not at all. The sound of his voice was drowning me in its richness. My shivers were the good kind, like when the guy of your dreams finally becomes brave enough to put his arm around you.

"Are you there, Kira?" the captain had to ask again.

"Affirmative," I said, wondering if, shivers or not, I should disconnect. I reached over to turn on the mike. I was going to ask the captain if I'd offended him the day before.

"I have dreamed of you," he said. "Twice."

I gasped for air. My elbow slipped and sent my pencil flying off the desk and rolling across the wooden floor. My eyes followed. The Natharan continued.

"In my dreams, your hair streams outward as if the wind is caressing each strand. Short wisps of curl flutter about your face like the leaves in a tree under a gentle breeze. I see the light of your yellow sun sparkling against each strand of your auburn hair, reflecting golden streaks of fire. I cannot clearly see your face. The forward motion of your hair blowing about covers your face teasingly. I strain to capture your image. In the dream, I can see that your eyes are bright with courage, and I imagine that your nose turns slightly upwards with a chin that is strong and well-formed. Yet, I cannot tell for sure.

"You are standing on a hill, Kira, and your slender body is being buffeted by increasingly fierce gusts of wind, and yet you are resistant. You do not bend or allow the wind to alter your stance. You are defiant.

"Both times, Kira, I have seen that same image in my dreams. My people are not far-seers. We do not have the ESP I have read of on your planet. Why do I see you in my dreams? What magic do you hold, my Kira?"

I would have spoken then, but I could barely breathe. The captain's voice was singing in my ears. His words had taken me far away. I was standing at the top of that hill, looking down. I could feel the wind on my cheeks. My hair was blowing all about me and kept flinging itself across my eyes. I wanted to reach out and take hold of it with my hands, so I could see more clearly, but I couldn't move. Desperately, I sought to catch a glimpse of the Natharan at the bottom of that hill. I closed my eyes, trying to visualize his face, fighting for the vision.

Once more, the captain began to speak. I opened my eyes. My plasto-wood desk still held a half-empty can of cola. I swallowed a restorative gulp.

"It is said that your planet holds witches, Kira — witches who cast their spells on men and sirens that sing hauntingly sweet melodies to lure males to them. Which one are you, Kira — a siren or a witch?"

He was the one who was the enchanter! I must have been in shock, or perhaps I was hysterical. I don't know why I did it. I broke all training when the Natharan said that about sirens and witches. I'd just flipped on the transystem to answer him . . . and then I burst out in laughter. It was inexcusable.

We'd been trained in our work with alien cultures that laughter was often misconstrued. After all, how could you explain "funny"? It was like the expression we have on Earth: "You had to be there to understand." Most cultures not only didn't understand laughter, they were offended by it. So I knew better.

When I was able to control myself and stop, I apologized over and over, but the Natharan didn't seem upset. He waited until I was through with my flood of "sorries," and then he said with the sweetest, most gentle voice, "Do not express regret, Kira. I am most delighted with your laughter. It has explained everything. I know now what you are."

I leaned forward. The captain's voice was so low and quiet I was afraid I wouldn't catch every word he said.

"You are a siren, Kira. Your voice and your laughter, they call to me. I am your captive, Earth Siren."

My ears were ringing. I felt dizzy. I found that I was biting at my lower lip. I picked up my diet soda can and then held it against my mouth. The cold only numbed my lips. It didn't help my nerves.

There was magic in the captain's words. I closed my eyes and sighed. My spine was warm and tingly. I could almost feel the warmth of his breath touching my neck. If only this guy were human . . .

But he wasn't.

"I have to get back to work," I blurted out. Without pausing to hear his reply, I flipped off the switch. I was shaking. My hand, as it reached out to pick up the soda can, could barely close around the slippery surface. I drew in several calming breaths, finished my drink, and sat, too upset to work.

The caterpillar clock was purring steadily, unbothered by aliens and transystem calls. I listened to its rhythm as I closed my eyes. It was a sound I rarely heard, the gentle "cha, cha, cha." It was so soft a movement and so soothing, I relaxed into it.

When I was calmer, I opened my eyes. I'd rested only a moment. The caterpillar had barely moved. It wasn't yet time to go home. I knew I should turn my transline back on, but there were plenty of other offices like mine with people handling the calls. The system could do without me another moment.

I started to stand up and take a break. Maybe I'd feel better if I washed my face in the washroom or bought a Nutribar from the machine across the hall. But the thought of facing others made me feel nauseous. I planted my elbows on the desk and cupped my chin.

I could almost hear again the melodious baritone of the captain. How could it haunt me so? Why did I feel half-hypnotized by his words? How could words alone create this yearning in me?

I could still picture the dream, as vivid as a memory. Was it possible to meet in dreams? How could the captain know those things about me? Did I have a strong chin? My father said I did. And my nose turned up, but only a little. Did the captain only guess that I was slender? Had I told him how long my hair was?

I jerked open my desk drawer and started to pop another tran-laxer for my pounding head, but then I remembered I'd already taken two that morning. I shut the drawer and closed my eyes.

Almost immediately, I was seeing myself on the hill the Natharan had spoken of. There were flowers in the grass, small yellow ones like marigolds — no, more like tiny, miniature sunflowers. Their fragrance was of honeysuckle. I breathed in deeply.

Then, I panicked and bolted upright. There was no hill, no flowers. I was in my office. Why had I thought I smelled honeysuckle? It took a moment before my mind, and my eyes registered that I was staring at the poster on the wall, the one I'd brought from my bedroom at home.

The poster was the first thing I'd tacked up in my office when I came to New York. Funny how I used to think that growing up meant leaving behind the familiar things from childhood. But when I got my job at Transline-System, I brought my favorite poster.

I studied it as if I'd never seen it before. My father would have said it was just a picture of a horse and its rider. But it was so much more. It was from the Grand Championship Jumping Exhibition, and the horse, a black thoroughbred named Nightmagic, had just vaulted up. His forelegs were pawing empty space as if he were able to climb the air. His body was stretched, hurtling forward by the force of his will. His hind hooves had just departed from the ground, pushing him forward and vertically. He was frozen in that magical second when gravity didn't seem to exist.

The horse's rider, Marlene Davees, sat on the gelding's back with perfect form. Her body was an unbroken line that extended from her hands and arms clear down to her seat. You could tell that the contact she held through the fingers in her reins to the bit in Nightmagic's mouth was light and flexible. Even her legs and thighs pressed just so for absolute control, and connection spoke of the faultless communication between horse and woman.

I sighed. Spending time looking at my poster had always calmed me before. Only this time, gazing at Nightmagic didn't help. I could still hear the Natharan's voice calling me his Earth Siren.

"This is ridiculous," I said out loud. Why should I care what some alien called me? I'd seen aliens at SpacePort many times since I'd moved to the city. Long-nosed, antennaed, green and purple, google-eyed, winged, ugly, ethereal, tall, thin, broad. Visiting SpacePort was like walking through a zoo, an intergalactic one, with mixed-up body parts assembled on creatures that breathed and babbled in squeaks and hisses. I wasn't one of those girls who hung around there looking for the novel "beastie" just to sample interstellar relationships. Alien bodies didn't fascinate me nor draw me to them. Most of them made me want to close my eyes until they passed.

Yet, I'd never seen a Natharan. What did the captain look like? How repulsive could he be when he called me a siren and spoke of how I'd captivated him?

A call came in then. I was glad. The routine kept me from thinking about the captain.

During my afternoon break, I headed for the Transline-Center Library. I might as well have joined the others for a drink at Qwerl's Cafeteria. The library was a waste of time. There were no pictures of Natharans in the *Official Intergalactic Encyclopedia*. In fact, there was almost no information about the planet Natharan at all.

All known species were contained in that book. There were pictures of home worlds, information on cultural activities, governments, education, religions, policies, and restrictions, and even some interactive language tapes. Most of the alien cultures took whole chapters to discuss, but the *Encyclopedia* only contained one paragraph about the Natharan, and in that paragraph, all I learned was that Natharans were reclusive. They refused to be photographed or to provide data about their planet or species. Information from other sources only provided the added information that Natharans were nonviolent.

I was irritated by the lack of info on them, but my research made me even more curious. If Natharans were reclusive, why was the captain so friendly? Why was he so open and so anything *but* shy and reserved? Curiosity stabbed at my good sense. I kept telling myself not to get involved, but if the captain called again, I knew I'd listen. Who could turn away from such a mystery?

That night, I dreamed of the mysterious space captain. But my dream was nothing like the Natharan's. Mine was a nightmare, and my fear molded him grotesquely. He had huge, fuzzy, molting antlers that dripped sulphur-yellow slime. His muzzle as he peered at me with his tiny yellow eyes, was bulldoggish, wrinkled, and puckered. And he was squatty, coming only up to my breasts.

I kept worrying that the alien would come too close and stab me with his antlers or drip slime on my shoes. At one point in my dream, he tried to pick me up to carry me back to his ship, but I was bigger than he was, and I bopped him on the head with my purse. It was a stupid dream — not scary, but not what I'd call pleasant either.

Later, in my tiny office (four walls that formed a perfect square, no bigger than an apartment's washroom,) I was still recovering from the dream when the Natharan called. With that nightmare still fresh in my mind, I wasn't as friendly to his overtures, no matter how warm and sexy his voice was.

My hand shook as I reached for my diet soda, but I listened, and when the elegance of his words swayed my resolve, I purposefully recalled my nighttime vision. The remembrance of those beady, yellow eyes and the mucous slime he'd drooled on me in my dream helped me to steel my mind to the captain's deep, rich baritone. The Natharan must have realized that his words were no longer enchanting me. He stopped and said, "Kira, tell me about you."

It was not the right thing to say. I hate people who say, "Tell me about you." First of all, you never know what to say. Then, you finally figure out something that's not too stupid, and you start to speak. Your mind begins remembering it, visualizing it as if it were happening all over again, and you get so involved with that memory that it becomes special to you.

You start to feel a sudden bonding with the person you're sharing it with. So you look up into their eyes, hoping to see a new closeness, a connection . . . and you realize that the eyes of the person who asked for that piece of you are scooting around like a runaway top, and you see that he's thinking about dinner or politics or what that spot is on the carpet.

It makes you feel diminished, flattened, worse than the spot on the carpet because you see that the something of value that you've pulled up from deep inside you where you store the essence of your soul — that creep doesn't even think it's worthy of a moment's listening.

I despise that feeling. It's like the person is rejecting the depths of your soul. And now, this alien creature, who probably looked like a cross between a garbage heap and vomit with earrings, was asking me to risk it. I know I overreacted to his request. I should have been more understanding. I should have explained how I felt, but there were too many hurts and too many failures from living in the city. I shrieked at the Natharan like it was his fault. "Go plug it in your ear!" I yelled.

I could have lost my job for that. I would have if the captain had complained to Mr. Dee, but he only got very quiet for a moment, and then he explained that Natharans didn't need earplugs because their ears had a natural protection against high decibels.

I don't know what the translator made out of my sigh. I was upset and shaken by my rudeness. I'd never lost my temper on the transline before, and I couldn't understand what had made me yell at the captain.

He didn't wait for me to "pull myself together." He just started talking. "I withdraw the request, Kira. I believe it has affected you disagreeably. But may I ask . . . how have my words offended you?"

The captain was so sweet. He hadn't deserved what I'd said. I owed him an explanation. I tried to explain about people who never listened and about how their rejection makes you feel inside. I could tell that he was listening as I meandered through apologies and rationalizations. He had a way of saying my name with such gentleness, like an urging for me to continue talking.

Intuitively, I knew that he wouldn't judge me nor find my thoughts and feelings dull or trite. And when he repeated my name like that, with his voice low and quiet, calm and encouraging, almost like a soft purr, it told me that he understood everything I was saying. His acceptance eased my pain.

But other than those soothing, soft-voiced encouragements, he said nothing. Even when I paused to catch my breath or reshape the words to fit how I was feeling, he didn't rush in to speak. He let me talk until I emptied out my unhappiness.

When I was through, I thanked him for listening and for not being angry at my rudeness. He was silent for several minutes. My heart speeded up, and uncertainty began to trickle back. Should I have spoken so openly? Suppose the Natharan was insulted by something? What if I was wrong about him? What if he judged me and found me flawed? What if . . .

When, at last, he spoke, I knew the depth of his listening. The Natharan had listened almost too well.

"You have been hurt, Kira," he said. "Your words and intonation carry your pain. It stabs at me. I cannot take away the anguish that you feel within you. All I can do is give you my promise that I will never harm you in that way."

My eyes were starting to tear, and the hurt inside me felt like it was trying to rise up and bubble out of me. Somehow, it got stuck in my throat, and I coughed to free it, and then the pain erupted, not in a sob, but in a burst of rage. I flung the anger and the fear at that poor Natharan. "In what way *will* you harm me?" I cried out.

Perhaps I was already building my defense against the coldness of the city. Natharans call it "the Terran's learning-not-to-trust syndrome." The Natharan captain slipped underneath that shield. He recognized the anger in my voice, yet he wasn't insulted. He answered me as earnestly as if I'd asked him why the sky was blue.

"Ah, Kira, if ever I were to hurt you, it would be through my ignorance, as I did when I asked you to tell me of yourself. Earth Siren, I would never intentionally bring you harm."

My hand jerked closed, and the aluminum can I was holding was crushed in the center. Soda erupted all over my jeans. The soda was diet, so at least my legs wouldn't be sticky, but my lap was soaking wet. I threw the can into the trash and looked about for something to clean up with.

I tugged a wad of tissues from the plastic box on my desk and told the Natharan abruptly that I had to go, that I had work to do. Then I blotted at my jeans and tried to calm my nerves.

How could an alien do this? How could he understand me so well? How did he know just the right thing to say?

"This is ridiculous," I said aloud, although there was, luckily, no one around to hear. "How can I believe an alien is sympathetic? He can't even imagine what a human needs. He can't know that much about us, and he certainly can't understand me. So how can he do this? Why does he do it? What does he want from me?"

I stood up to pace. My pants and legs were wet. In the temperature-regulated room, I felt cold. I pulled my jacket off the hook on the wall and thrust my arms into it. It did not cover my legs, but its bulkiness comforted me.

Why was the Natharan so perfect? It wasn't possible for another human to understand me. How could an alien be so perceptive and kind? It had to be a trick. But what if he weren't a fake? What if the captain really possessed that much sensitivity? What if he truly cared about how I felt? What if he is as wonderful as he seems?

My head reeled with doubts. I shook it and started to laugh. My thoughts reminded me of one of those old songs my dad kept around. Wasn't there a plastic disk that scratchily crooned, "The man of my dreams is an alien"? If not, if my memory was playing tricks on me, perhaps I could write the lyrics. Maybe it would sell a million.

Calls interrupted my musings. Then, after I'd had time for a good laugh at myself, I started thinking about how rude I'd been to the Natharan. If he weren't up there on that ship hatching a nefarious scheme for which he needed a human victim, then I was an utter fool. I should never have demanded that he tell me how he was planning to hurt me. And why had I said that? The Natharan had actually never said an unkind word.

I made endless resolutions not to talk with the captain again. Then, I changed my mind and vowed that I would call him one more time just to apologize. And after that, I'd never talk with him again. My mind argued, and I waged long discourses with the silent walls. The framed poster of Nightmagic stared down at me. Sometimes, the horse appeared to be laughing at me or at the silliness of humans. But what did he know frozen forever in that perfect moment of freedom?

Chapter Three: Definition of Alien, *Strange*

For two days, there was electrical interference between the captain and me that the transystem couldn't override. The guilt I carried tortured my days and my dreams. I went to work, I did my job, I laughed and joked with the others, but a part of me kept viewing everything from a distance. Inside me, a voice repeatedly said, "How would the Natharan view this? What would he say?"

I called my dad. We talked. I couldn't fool him. He knew at once that something was bothering me. He kept asking what was wrong. How could I answer? Nothing was wrong. I just felt different.

When finally, the Natharan was able to get through, I had things to say that poured from my mouth. He let me talk, and when my storm of apology ended, he said, "Kira, my siren, fear and anger erect walls that are not there. The offense was only in your mind."

I felt like crying. The captain was so unbelievably sweet. No matter what I said, he didn't become upset with me. He only tried to understand. How different he was from everyone I knew! How wonderful!

I knew it then. It was like sunshine breaking through the clouds. The gray gloom and chill of the past two days were instantly gone. I was warmed by the knowledge that my Natharan cared.

Words flew off my tongue before I could curb them. "Captain, what color is your hair? How old are you? What is your marital status?" I'd asked him nothing before, not seeking involvement. Now, my curiosity was overflowing.

Natharans don't laugh, he'd told me, but amusement was curled around his words so thickly I could almost see his smile. "I am Cegan. Will you say my name, Earth siren?"

"Cegan."

"Thank you, Kira. It is music spoken from your lips.

"My hair is gold. I am . . . it would be about thirty of your years. I have no mate, nor am I yet promised to one."

He wasn't married! Why should I care? Yet the fact sang ripples of joy in my heart. The captain, Cegan, was a lot older than I was. No wonder he was so wise. Thirty was a good age. A perfect age for a man! Absolutely perfect!

I wanted to dance or twirl round and round on top of my desk. My fingers clasped the sides of my chair. Keep me from flying, I wanted to tell them. Keep me anchored to the world, or I shall float upwards towards the mysterious, wonderful space captain.

My brain was a wheel in a mouse's cage, running in circles. Faster and faster flew my thoughts. I reached out for one. My voice was on an automatic. It responded with a calmness I found amazing. "Gold! Your hair is gold? Not yellow? Gold, all in one color, like the metal?"

"All one color, like the metal," he said.

I sighed. Gold hair seemed to fit the voice I knew. Yet what else went with that dreamy baritone that sang to me in my dreams?

"Please tell me what you look like, Cegan," I begged, hardly able to breathe as I waited to hear. There was a silence. A long silence. How could he stop speaking? My heart was beating faster than my brain. My brain had frozen still, locked on that one question. Didn't he know how important it was? What did he look like?

Please, tell me, please, my mind begged silently. But the Natharan's silence went on and on. Would he never answer? Would he disconnect and never call again? I wanted to scream at him, "Answer!" Yet, inside me, a voice said, *Wait. Give him time.*

I shut my eyes and listened to the sounds around me. The clock on the wall, scratching its way around the hour, and the tiny groan just before it forced its small hand to budge another millimeter. They were the only distractions in the soundproofed room — besides the beating of my heart, booming its anxiety.

"I think," the captain said, at last, "that you want me to tell you how our species differ."

Yes! I breathed again. Yes, tell me.

"But I believe, Kira, that you and I should focus on what we have in common."

That would be nice, I almost said, but I bit my lips closed, ignoring the pain of a mouth parched dry from tension.

"Natharans, like Terrans, have a brain in their head and all the same sense organs in more or less the same locations."

As if I had a paper before me and a pencil in hand, my mind began to sketch.

"We walk on feet attached to legs. We have arms and hands of the same number."

My mental sketch was sending relief. Cegan was a person, not a squid or a fat eight-legged spider sitting on his spaceship web.

"Our bodies are of similar sizes."

Similar! He could mean he was four feet tall. Could I date a man a foot shorter than I was?

"Are you relieved now, Kira?" he asked.

No! I needed to know so much more. What did his face look like? How many fingers did he have? Were his feet webbed? Did he wear clothes like us? What was his body wrapped in? Bark? Or an exoskeleton like an insect?

I could feel the alien's hesitation. Why did he not wish to discuss what he looked like? Was he so ugly that he feared I would be repulsed? "Captain, Cegan, do we look alike?" I hedged.

"We are similar in body appearance, Kira, but, no, Terrans and Natharans are not alike." He paused a moment as if thinking. "Kira, that part does not truly matter. Our souls are equal. We are both beings of consciousness and intelligence. In that regard, we are alike. Should bodies be more important than souls?"

He was right. But, it did matter to me what he looked like. I wanted to see him, desperately, to know if I could like the body that went with the mind. I wasn't a computer with wires for circuits. I needed to touch a hand that was warm and see into eyes that responded to mine.

I badgered him for more information. He was patient and gentle in his refusals, but he would tell me nothing more about his appearance. "Our souls are the same," he kept repeating.

That night, I endeavored to construct a picture from Cegan's statements. But all I could achieve was a faceless blur. The captain had said that he had a nose, a mouth, eyes, and ears, but how were they assembled? It was only minute differences that made human faces individual.

How much larger or smaller or askew could a facial part be before we deemed it hideous? Yet, did it really matter? Should it matter? His response to my pleading for more details did have a rightness to it. It was true that souls reaching out to each other had a nice sound to it, but for a human, at least, it certainly wasn't very satisfying.

Cegan always spoke about ideas and beliefs, and I respected the things he said, but my imaginings were still filled with ugly monsters. Sometimes, in my dreams, they read poetry to me or chased me around the transystem offices, and lately, I'd had a recurring one, something from *Beauty and the Beast*, except that when I married the beast, he never turned back into a prince. What would Beauty have done then? Would she still have kissed the Beast and taken him to her bed?

What did Cegan want with me, anyway? Maybe appearance was unimportant to him because I was only a friend who relieved the boredom of a long space flight. Did he think of me as more than a friend? When he called me his siren, didn't that imply something more?

He'd asked me once if I were married. Wasn't that significant? Of course, on Natharan, that question might be part of every introduction, for all I knew. But he'd dreamed about me, and once, he said that I'd captured him. Surely, those indicated more than friendship.

Yet, when I'd told Cegan how much I'd always wanted to travel to other worlds, he hadn't suggested that someday I might be welcome on his ship. It was too strange, and all the mystery about the Natharans made it even worse.

A refrain of queries clanked in and out of my thoughts, destroying the depths of my sleep, my rest, and my work. A sense of unease pricked my confidence. I knew I had to resolve my doubts. Perhaps my friends and acquaintances noticed nothing, but I felt unstable and unsure.

I wasn't willing to give up the conversations with my fascinating captain. But since Cegan resisted my probing about what he looked like, I decided to gather my own information about the alien and his planet, Natharan.

The next day at work, I called other captains. There were actually no company rules against using the transline for private conversation. If Mr. Dee or the other big wheels at the firm discovered it, I suppose I might be fired, but Transtel-programmers were in great demand, so maybe not.

And I guess it's possible, as a commentator later suggested, that I could have set off an interplanetary situation, but I didn't. Every captain I talked to that day was extremely friendly, and none of them seemed to mind my questions. The conversations were interesting, although some of them were very strange, but I didn't learn a single thing about Natharan or about the mysterious Captain Cegan.

"Can't you tell me anything about Natharans?" I kept asking each captain.

Several of them told me that Natharans were not fond of being talked about and that it would be better if we did not discuss their planet.

"What would they do to us?" I asked. There was apparently no answer to that question. "Would they hurt us?" I questioned.

All the captains were emphatically negative about that idea, but each of them persisted in reiterating that a discussion of Natharan would not be prudent.

I asked the captains if they knew anything about Captain Cegan. Once more, I was informed that it was better not to discuss anything related to Natharan. All I could learn was that they knew Cegan and that he was a member of their League of Traders.

Only two of the captains dared to volunteer anything. A Baskante told me that Natharans never lied, and a Qweldon bravely told me that

Natharans never fought. I half-expected to hear someone tell me that Natharans were secretive. It was as if they were holding a copy of the *Official Intergalactic Encyclopedia* and reading out of it.

All of the captains were very skillful evaders. Not only did they not answer a single question, but they also countered with their own and attempted to quiz me about my conversations with Cegan! Why should alien captains care about what Cegan and I discussed?

By the time I'd made contact with each of the seventy-eight captains on my transline, I was so irritated by my lack of progress I was pacing. Back and forth, back and forth. It helped my thinking, but I wished, as I always did, that my office was bigger, that the floor was a dirt path, and that I could once more jog my frustrations out on a trail underneath the open sky and tall trees.

I'd become so tense from the mystery of it, or should I say, the frustration, that I couldn't drink my diet colas. I was afraid of the caffeine. Another cup of coffee or a cola, and I knew I'd be climbing walls like Spider-Man. Then those men in the white coats would come for me, and I would tell them I was probably falling in love with an alien, and they'd nod their heads and smile at each other, then escort me out the door.

I sighed and dropped down into the heavy desk chair. The force of my body sent the chair rolling backwards on wheels that moved across the plasticized wooden floor. I kicked off the wall and pushed back to my desk.

I'd struck out badly with my research. I was discouraged and irritated with Cegan. It was a bad time to call him, but I couldn't concentrate on anything else. I didn't want him to know what I'd been doing all day. It was too much like spying, so I began babbling about a movie I'd seen recently with my friend Frances.

For the first time, he interrupted me. "Kira, I think that you are attempting to hide behind the flow of your words. What is it you wish to tell me?"

Why should that bring tears to my eyes? I gathered up tissues and wiped. My sniffling was the only break in the silence. "I don't want to tell you anything," I said a moment later, and I blew my nose loudly in annoyance.

Cegan didn't comment. I couldn't stand his silence. I answered him. "I don't want to tell you anything. I want to ask you things, but you always refuse to answer!"

"Is this the cause of your tears, Kira?"

"Yes, no," I said, standing up. I looked over at the speaker, trying to picture Cegan speaking into his. "It doesn't matter, Cegan," I said, wishing I could pace again. "But all the mystery surrounding you, Natharans, is maddening!

"I can't sleep wondering why you can't just tell me!" I broke off then. I was too unsure of Cegan to say more. I still didn't know what would anger him or make him choose never to talk with me again.

As usual, he was silent for a while, pondering my words. I bit at my fingernail, where a jagged edge was annoying me. I nibbled it off.

"Natharans are not evasive without purpose, Kira. You must believe that."

"Why?" I snapped back before he'd barely gotten the words delivered across the transline.

"Without trust, siren, there are no answers."

I thought about that for a moment. "Without answers, there is no trust."

"You delight me, my siren," he responded.

I stopped biting at my nails and turned to stare at the wall. If only I could see him. If only I could look into his eyes! Wouldn't I know *then* if I could trust him? I groaned softly and leaned my forehead against the roughness of the wall.

"There is tension in your voice and manner today, Kira. I think your calls to the others have only brought you disappointment."

I whirled around as if he were there behind me. My fingers rapidly flicked the switch on. "They told you?"

"Yes, they have informed me of your attempts to question them. You will not find Natharan in that direction, Kira."

I stamped my foot. "And you won't tell me about Natharan because it's this huge mystery that Terrans aren't allowed to know about, right?"

"Kira. Stop! Listen to me now. Will you do that for me? Will you promise me that no matter what I say to you, even if it is something you are not ready to hear, you will not simply turn off the transline and refuse to speak with me again? Will you give me your word on that, Kira, that you will call me tomorrow?"

I turned and gazed up at the ceiling. It brought me no closer to the elusive Cegan, but at least I was looking in his direction. "I don't understand. Are you about to tell me something awful? You can't expect me to promise if it is . . ."

"Kira! Trust me!"

He'd never yelled at me before. It stunned me into silence. I closed my eyes, and counted to five, then I kept on counting slowly. When I got to twenty-one, I opened my eyes and said softly, "I think I can trust you, Cegan. I promise to continue our discussions. I can't think of anything you could say that would make me not want to talk with you again."

He heaved a heavy sigh. "I knew you had it in you, Kira. Thank you for your trust."

I felt like I'd been congratulated for a job well done. I was suddenly dizzy and hot. I pushed up my shirtsleeves, then fanned myself. My lemon-lime soda can was empty, but I fought it for the last drop. I felt my forehead. My hand felt icy against its heat. The clock's caterpillar hand still dragged itself around the seconds, whining. Why was the clock suddenly so loud? Why wasn't Cegan talking? What was he waiting for?

"Kira," he said, and my heart jolted with a double beat.

"This artificial partition between us is no easier for me than it is for you, and I am extremely apprehensive that, despite your promise, I will frighten you away and you will disconnect us forever, but I cannot continue with your doubts like a xxxxx, gnawing away at my interior region. I am driven by something inside me to explain to you that I have fallen into a comet that has me churning into ever-widening, maddened cycles of . . ."

"You hit a comet, Cegan?" I cried out. "You're in danger!" My hand was centimeters from the alarm button. "Should I try to get help?" I cried out.

"No! Kira," Cegan said firmly. "Do not leave me, my sweet, sweet Kira. Remember your promise. Sit back down. I can hear that you are standing. Your chair is still reeling from your departure."

The chair was reeling because I'd knocked it askew getting back to the on-switch, but I didn't bother to explain. I steadied it and sat down. If there was no comet, what was Cegan talking about?

"Good. Now, relax, Kira. Breathe gently. This inadequate, malfunctioning xxxxx of a translator has not given you my meaning at all. There is no comet, my auburn-haired siren, no comet except for the one inside my heart that is driving me beyond all intelligence, making my waking moments an agony of doubt. What I am trying to tell you, my indescribably delightful Kira, is that I love you."

"You do?"

"Irrefutably."

"You can't. That's not possible. You don't know me. We're from different planets. We're different species. We're . . ."

"Hush, Kira," he crooned. "I hear the fear in your voice. Do not fear me, my siren."

I took a deep breath and held it, letting it out as slowly as I could. It didn't help me. I was still shaking.

"I will never hurt you, Kira."

"I'm not ready for this," I cried out.

"I know."

"I don't know what to say. I'm all mixed up."

"You do not need to say anything, Kira."

"I have to go home. I have to think."

"Promise me, Kira."

"What?" I croaked out, feeling tears flooding my eyes.

"Easy, Kira. Do not panic because I told you I love you. If you feel only friendship, we can still talk. Will you call me tomorrow? Will you promise me that, Kira?"

"Yes. I'll call you," I promised, and then I severed the line.

I know I should have said something more. I should have thanked Cegan, at least. Wasn't that what you did when a man told you he loved you? But Cegan wasn't a man.

I lay my head down on the desk, cradling my face in my arms. I think I moaned. I know, I cried. I was confused. I felt sick, but I couldn't get up to leave.

I'd wanted to hear Cegan tell me he loved me. I think I'd dreamed about it, but now his words left me disoriented. The room was spinning. Was that how it felt to be on his ship? My head was pounding. I felt disconnected from what was real.

An alien with beady, yellow eyes and seven-fingered hands loved me. What should I do? A drill in my head was boring down. My skin was burning. I barely made it to the plastic can. I emptied my stomach and then lay on the floor. It was not how I'd pictured such a romantic event.

In bed that night, I found no sleep. Could I love Cegan? Like an irritating jingle playing over and over, I couldn't escape the question. I knew how he felt about me, but did I return that love? Did I love Cegan?

I thought I would be sick the next morning, but I woke up hungry. I nibbled at a piece of toast and drank some herb tea. My eyes felt scratchy, but otherwise, I was well. I would have stayed home anyway, but I'd given Cegan my word. I had to call him, but what would I say?

I dressed without thinking, programmed by prior mornings. I arrived at the office at the usual time. I picked up a pencil and began to construct a grid: Pros and Cons. The pencil snapped on the 'o' of Cons. The pen was out of ink. I flipped the switch, and he was there.

"Good morning, siren. The hours of your night have been long. Did you find them so?

"Yes."

"We have shared the wait together, then. My eyes this night were often on the rotation of your planet. Did you not feel my gaze attempting to urge it faster? It is humbling to know how little the desire of one individual influences the cycles of a solar system. And how equitable that is! For had I possessed the power, I would have hastened morning, only concerned lest it bother you, ignoring the needs of billions of others."

"It would not have bothered me if the night were shorter. I couldn't sleep."

"And that is my fault. I am sorry, my Kira."

I heard him sigh. How is it that the sound of his frustration could be so human? I loved his sigh . . . and his thoughts . . . and how they were so much the echo of my heart. If he were only human, I *would* love him.

"I told you that I would not speak of Natharan, but it is so a part of me it is difficult to hold it away from you. I give you my trust, Kira, that you will never speak of it to others. The words for 'love' and for 'trust' are one word in Natharan."

"I won't speak of it. I promise, Cegan."

"I trust you, my siren. If you will permit it, I will take you with me to Natharan. Close your eyes now and listen to my words. You will be the first of your kind to peer beneath the 'Protector's Veil,' and we will welcome you, my Kira."

"What is a 'Protector's Veil'?"

31

"No questions, Kira. You must be silent to ride my words."

"To ride his words" — how could you not love such a man, I thought to myself. Then, I closed my eyes and let Cegan guide me to his world.

"Natharan is a large, green planet where water is abundant. From space, you will see no brown — only the dark green of forests and the emerald green of the smaller grasses and shrubs. There are many rivers — small blue paths that are like woven patterns in the green. And there are oceans, Kira — not blue as yours — but jade and turquoise. And lakes are far more plentiful on Natharan. They appear from space to be sapphires, shiny as mirrors in the light of the twin suns . . ."

"*Two* suns?"

"Kira, I cannot take you to Natharan if you insist on breaking the spell."

I didn't speak again. In a moment, he continued. "You will see mountains with snowcaps, my siren. They are not so high as your world's great peaks. Natharan is an older world, and the mountains, majestic and proud as they are, bend over slightly, bowed with their vast age. Their snow is like your white sugar icing, solid across the top and dripping down the sides. Do you see them, Kira?"

"Yes," I said, forgetting to be silent.

"Look to your right, Kira. Those are the flatlands. They extend for distances far greater than your continent of North America. It is there, in the gentle grasslands, that my family dwellings are found. Do you see the green all around you, Kira?"

"Yes," I said once more.

"We are bonded well, then. Ride further, my siren. I shall take you down to that grassy reach. Your shoes may become quite damp unless you are wearing boots. In the flatlands, mornings always hold moisture. A dense fog swells up from the ground and hovers about the buildings and plants. If you walk into it, you will lose your way, Kira. There are those who name this a sport, and they set forth each morning, pushing through the mists. They wear an electronic guard so they do not harm their limbs from collision with unseen obstacles, and they stroll madly, blindly about, and have no idea where their walking will take them.

"I had always believed their sport to be a ridiculous one, Kira. Yet, last night, after you left, I closed my eyes, and I imagined you here with me on Natharan, walking into that mist. It does not seem unreasonable to me now, Kira. With our hands touching and the rest of the world an oblivion of whiteness, it seems like a great adventure, a pleasurable one. You would enjoy such a challenge, wouldn't you?

"Open your eyes now, my siren, for I am forced to return you to your Earthly home. But answer me this, my Kira — if I take you up in my ship one day, will you be brave enough to walk in the mists of Natharan with me?"

I wanted to, but Cegan was right to ask if I had the courage. I didn't know if I would be daring enough even to hold his hand.

And so the days continued. I, never making a commitment, avoided every discussion of how I felt, and Cegan, who risked it all: his heart, his trust, the outer layer of his secret world, and his inner thoughts. A Natharan believes that patience is a part of integrity, but even a Natharan must have doubts that patience will not always triumph. If that were true of Cegan, he hid his doubts well.

Janna, a woman with an office three doors down from mine, was pregnant and due at the end of the month. When she went into labor,

I was called late in the evening to come in on the following day. It was no problem for me to work on my day off. As I usually did, I left my apartment and arrived at work early so I could talk to Cegan on the transline before starting my mandatory calls. But when I opened our connection, Cegan didn't chime in with his usual "Good morning."

It bothered me that he wasn't there. After all, where else could he be? And then, when I kept checking the connection, and there was still no Cegan, I began to worry. Wouldn't one of the crewmen take over if Cegan were ill? In a true emergency, the second-in-command could make contact with us. Yet, no one answered the indicator light. I turned the connection on and off several times, praying that there wasn't some kind of malfunction, but all the circuits registered full variance.

It was early to start making my other calls, but I needed something to do to stop myself from fretting. I couldn't ask about my Natharan, of course, because it was Janna's line-up, but I think, in the back of my mind, I was hoping that one of her captains might mention if Cegan's ship had had a problem.

I plotted in all the first cluster's coordinates, and everyone except one of the Qweldons was correctly aligned on the grid. I ran the Qweldon's new calculations through the charting program and sent him out the amended position. When that was completed, I left Janna's room then checked Cegan's output from my own transline. Cegan came on the line.

"Where have you been?" I asked. Then I flushed because I sounded like a jealous shrew.

"Are you all right, Kira?" Cegan asked as our lines crossed.

Transmissions could never be simultaneous. That wasn't possible. What had happened to the on/off switch? We didn't stop to discuss it right then. It was much later that Cegan admitted that he'd accidentally revealed a Natharan technology. I promised secrecy, and from then on, we no longer used the on/off switch.

But that was later, as I said. First, there were the assurances to be exchanged that all was well. I explained about Janna and coming in on my day off, and Cegan told me that he'd been in the ship's gym and shower, not bothering to check the light because he'd thought I wouldn't be calling that day.

"Shower and gym? We have those on our ships, as well. I viewed one last month at the Space Show. Are all ships the same then?"

"In general, Kira. Of course, there are some variations, such as the size of the chambers and the fact that certain species require different specifications."

"Like what?"

"Kira, it would be better if we tabled some of your questions until things are different between us."

"Meaning I'm only a Terran, and you're an all-knowing but secretive Natharan?"

"Your teeth are sharp, my siren."

"And?"

"Kira."

How did he make me feel guilty with just one word? "Which part of it did you object to?"

He sighed. "Kira, when there is perfect Trust between us, I will be able to answer your questions and discuss a hundred other things that quick brain of yours is so eager to learn."

This time, it was I who sighed heavily. I felt like a brat. "I'm sorry. I had no right to be demanding of you, Cegan."

He breathed in sharply. It was a very nonhuman — a whistled inhale, more like a dolphin's high-pitched call. "Ah, siren," he said. "I would tell you the layout of a hundred ships in exchange for the pledge of your love."

I still could not offer him that. So we talked instead of a book he'd just finished, one from a Terran author that I'd never read.

I ate lunch with my friend Frances that day, as I often did, and she told me all about the latest love of her life, a man named Ivy. He worked for the government and was trying to get her to change jobs and move into his building.

"Ivy? Isn't that a woman's name?" I asked her.

Frances burst out laughing. "I don't give a rap what his name is. Ivy's got what no woman ever had, Kira, and he uses it very nicely. How about you? Any new waxed candles in your life?"

I changed the subject and became very interested in my yogurt and fries. Frances obligingly began to analyze the merits of shopping at Crool's vs. Perter's. Not having been to either of them yet, I was given all the pertinent details.

For the rest of the week, I kept as busy as I could, trying not to dwell on the lack of a "waxed candle" in my life and struggling to persuade myself that I could not be in love with an alien who probably didn't even have one. Or did he? I shuddered to think what an alien's "waxed candle" might look like.

Keeping busy so I couldn't dwell on such things took a lot of energy. I called my dad and was thanked for the sweater I'd sent him. I watched a TD movie and played Spiril with my roommate. I painted my toenails in rainbows. I baked cookies for the office. And, on my days off, I visited the zoo, explored the Natural History Museum, checked out the nearest branch of the library, and even toured the Guggenheim Art Museum. Mostly, I just tried to pretend that everything was the same.

It was strange that no one suspected how bizarre my life had become. People walked by me on the streets and never looked back to take a second look. To them, I looked as normal as any other New Yorker. Why could nobody see how lost and confused I was? None of them stopped and tried to peek inside my head, but when I closed my eyes, I could picture it. My poor, befuddled brain was spinning like oatmeal being stirred round and round.

I made an effort to spend breaks with my office friends, participating in the chitchat that was our usual fare: comparing lipstick, a nail color, or discussing a movie we'd seen, but sometimes it seemed like I was only wasting time, waiting for the hour I could talk with Cegan again.

Frances looked at me strangely. I think she suspected that something was up, but mostly she laughed, and told me that my thoughts were too much "up there in the clouds." "Stop thinking so much," she'd say. "Life is for loving. Why don't you get yourself some and relax?"

I couldn't tell her about Cegan. I couldn't tell anyone. Frances, like all the New York friends I'd made, seemed to concentrate on the physical part of romance. She kept telling me that loving was cheaper than a gym membership and a heck of a lot more fun.

I couldn't argue with her beliefs. Frances sparkled with life, and she seemed to have more fun than anyone I'd ever met. She was always trying new things and wearing clothes more outrageous than even those my roommate Cathy wore. And Frances was always the envy of the office staff because her nights were full of new men.

Perhaps the others didn't rotate players quite as frequently, but from what I'd determined in listening, they all agreed with Frances' motto. How could I disclose to Frances, or to any of them, that the one I was falling in love with spoke of souls uniting, not bodies?

They'd all laugh at me. Then, they'd stare at me with that sick fascination that people have when someone's wearing live plants in their hair or has factory-dyed their skin a strange color. I didn't want to be thought of as weird, yet I felt different.

Maybe it was my father's training or being from a small town, or maybe I was just more of a romantic than I knew, but I wanted more than they did. I wanted what Cegan promised: the bonding of minds, the sharing of hearts, the union of souls.

I wanted that so much that sometimes I found myself thinking that *only* the hours I spent with Cegan had value. The rest of my life seemed like a distanced passivity where I watched the flow of time meandering through all the conversations around me.

"Did you hear what Bently, that talk show host, said about men who could not commit to one woman?"

"Imagine wearing shoes that color!"

"Are you sure I don't look fat in this dress?"

"Is Carlos, the waiter at the restaurant at the corner, really gay?"

"Did you hear about Ceedee's new man?"

I caught myself judging my friends as if I were superior somehow. That wasn't Cegan's influence. That wasn't his manner at all. He'd accept my friends and their opinions. He wouldn't make the kind of comparisons I was making in my struggle to clear my thinking. I wanted back what I was losing. I needed normality.

That weekend, I at last agreed to go to a "get-together" with my roommate. I'd been to a small party when I'd first arrived in the city, and since then, I'd never wanted to go to another. To be truthful, that party had shocked me so much that I'd actually considered returning home to the farm. But how could I base every New York party on one bad experience? At least, that's what Cathy kept saying.

Every Friday night was party night for her. She seemed to live for them. It was where she met all her boyfriends and, according to Cathy, had the "most incredible conversations with everyone important in New York." At the party I'd gone to, I hadn't heard many stimulating conversations, but Cathy was right, one time wasn't a fair judgment.

I couldn't believe how happy she sounded when I finally said I'd go. With a stomach writhing with the little worms of fear and doubt, I slipped on my dress, combed my hair, and tried not to think about what the night would bring.

I waited for Cathy in the small room we called a living room. It contained our kitchen on one wall, with the computer terminal, translinevision/music center, and all of our books on the other. The opposite sides held only the door leading out into the hall, with its bolts and alarms, and the two doors that led off into Cathy's bedroom and mine. The living room was too small for a couch, but it did have the chairs from our kitchen table, which took up most of the space. I sat on one of those chairs and watched the ceiling projections.

There were mostly news broadcasts playing. It didn't look like much was happening, so I called out for it to mute: the police were "coptering" after a speeder in one panel, another showed a new addition to the train terminal, a soap opera star was bawling about something in a third, and the fourth was a debate about some political issue that was obviously important to the individuals involved. I watched their mouths move and listened to Cathy singing a honky-tonk rap.

Cathy's bedroom door was open. I could see from where I was sitting that she was still trying on clothes. Two pantsuits were lying on the floor, and the dress she'd just snuggled into went flying over her head onto the bed. A loud zip announced the try-on of another. She noticed my gaze and twirled around, swishing the skirt of one of her newest purple satin dresses. Its v-neck was long enough to show her belly button and give peek-a-boo of most of the rest of her.

"What do you think, Kira? Does it make me look too fat?"

Cathy was beautiful. She had a perfect figure and all the height I lacked. Her hair, still uncombed yet perfectly shaped, swirled around her chin and neck. I envied Cathy's height, it was true, but it was Cathy's hair that I coveted. Her hair was the softest gold-streaked brown, probably the exact color of the material Rumpelstiltskin wove from straw.

I looked back up at the ceiling. "Your dress is beautiful, Cathy, and you couldn't look fat if you wore a barrel around your middle." I watched as the soap opera heroine flung herself into the arms of the most gorgeous man on Earth. His bulging arms were as wide as my thighs. I held my breath to see if the material in his shirt would tear from the strain. I never got to see it. The actress' hands rose up and covered the bulges. I could almost feel the hardness of the man's muscles under the woman's fingers.

Cathy rushed in then, completely destroying my concentration. "What do you think of this one?" she asked me as she paraded about.

I blinked and attempted to wrench my eyes from Mr. Gorgeous as his lips were embedding themselves in those of the star.

"How can you watch that trash?" Cathy whined. "Change panel 1," she ordered, and Mr. Gorgeous turned into a quiz show.

I discovered that I'd been biting my lip again. I opened my mouth to protest the loss of the hunk, but Cathy probably wouldn't have heard. She was berating me about not wearing something more daring.

"That is so unmod," she told me, looking over my dress. "Why don't you wear my new purple? Or borrow one of the others? You know I won't mind."

There was nothing wrong with the dress I had on. It was a pale violet, with inlays of crystalline polyester. Where I came from, it was even slightly risqué, but I had to admit it was tame compared with Cathy's. The crimson "dress" that she'd decided to wear had slits on all sides, from the breasts down. Cathy, like most city women, didn't wear underwear so every move she made showed a great deal of skin. I blushed and looked away.

"I can't wear one of yours, Cathy. I'm too short. Besides, even if something of yours did fit me, I wouldn't be able to. My dad would have a fit. He'd jerk me back home so fast I wouldn't have time to say goodbye."

Cathy clicked her tongue. "He doesn't have to know, Kira. You're an adult, remember?"

Cathy shook her head and stared at my dress. She was probably mentally surveying her own wardrobe, trying to think of something I could wear that would fit.

"Are you ready to go?" I asked, standing up and walking towards the door. I was not about to exchange my dress or anything else just so I could fit into what city-dwellers thought was the latest fashion.

Cathy shrugged, reapplied her lipdye, and checked the mirror one more time. "I'm ready," she said. As we turned to bolt the door and turn on the alarms, she added, "You know, Kira, you really do have a great figure. You don't need to hide it."

41

"Thank you," I said for the part of that which was supposed to be a compliment.

We started down in the elevator, but since we lived on the sixty-fourth floor, we had a ways to go. It gave Cathy time to go on with her lecture. "You know what my mom always says, Kira?"

I smiled. Her mom had quite a few juicy sayings. I wondered which one I was about to hear this time.

Cathy took my smile for interest and continued. "She always says that if you want to create a new relationship, you have to give it a catalyst. Do you get it, Kira? This dress is the catalyst."

Cathy continued in the same vein the whole way down. I shut out most of it and thought about how grateful I was that she'd worn a coat over the crimson dress. Our patrolled garage was probably safe, but it was always better not to attract too much attention.

The party was in a swank penthouse suite, about ninety floors up. One of the managers of sales from some big company was hosting the swang. As we got off the elevator, you could already hear the sound of partying: the music with its deep, hard-thumping sound that probably was supposed to give you ideas for the after and/or during the revelry's recreation, the laughter and talk of a hundred or more voices with the slightly hysteric quality that drugs and alcohol bring, and then as we stood outside the door, the general background noise of jingling bracelets, clinking glass, the crackling of well-maintained synthetic leather, and the tramping of so many feet against the soft, richly padded carpet.

We entered through huge double doors. I reached up and touched the side. Was it real wood? Money can even fake that.

As the door closed behind us, the increased noise level was an assault on my eardrums. I still hadn't become conditioned to the city dweller's need for loud noise. The smell of so many fragrance-enhanced bodies standing about in a range of colors and exposed skin tones was another affront to my tolerance level.

Cathy waved goodbye. Females did not stay together at parties in the city. They prowled through the room, searching for desirable males. We'd find each other when it was time to go. I watched Cathy slide through the mingled horde. Her dress didn't stand out at all. She was right. It was my dress that was far too modest.

I leaned my back against the entryway and surveyed the room. The walls were done in a white so luminous it was like looking at the moon on a dark, cold night. All the furniture was black leather and silver chrome, and the mirrors on the tops of tables, on the ceiling, and on every wall reflected it all back. I liked it. It worked.

I left my leaning post and continued on into the room, steering in the opposite direction from Cathy's departure. The night was still early. Few had paired off yet. Despite the timidity of my dress, I felt the eyes of several males scanning my body. One man with slightly greased-down hair and an orange robe-like toga began to tell me about his ex-girlfriend. Danny explained how Carola had been unimaginative and the possessor of zero creativity. It wasn't long before I learned that Carola had also not been a good bed partner, and Danny was, therefore, in search of another.

Timothy was the next man I met. He told me about his job writing articles for the *Daily Businessperson*. Timothy was more sophisticated than Danny, and his blue jeans were a nice touch. I think I would have liked listening about his research into stock analysis, but five minutes into his monologue, he stopped suddenly and demanded of me that I rate my degree of interest in him. He wasn't bad looking. His eyes were the kind of hazel that changes with the color of clothing worn. I would have liked to observe that change, but five minutes wasn't enough conversation for me to rate anything. I moved on.

I talked with Bob, James, and Tennyson. Each of them gave me a part of themselves, as Cegan would have said. But the part they shared was of soccer or cars or the career that didn't seem important enough to them to be a focus in their lives. None of them asked about me or seemed the least bit interested in what I did or felt.

I meandered through the groups for some time, keeping my eyes down to avoid unwanted contact, attempting only to listen to the flow of words. Nowhere did I hear anything of depth: no politics, no philosophy, no inner soul searching, only casual name exchanges and sexual innuendo.

As I progressed through the auditorium-sized room, I further admired the owner's taste. The black leather couches had all been pushed against the walls. They were overflowing with people yet seemed sturdy enough to handle it. The mirrors on the walls sparkled from the reflection of candle chandeliers that looked so real they flickered as they burned. Each mirror had been outlined with miniature fairy-like white Christmas bulbs, and the abundance of light in and on the mirrors opened up the room, making it seem even larger than it actually was.

I liked the touch of flowers the owner had placed in each corner. Huge earthenware pots of long-stemmed orchids with vivid saffron, fuchsia, and indigo blooms filled the angular spaces. I walked closer and breathed in the fragrance appreciatively. I was surprised to discover that only the purples were scented. The saffron orchids were not real.

The usual robot servers carried drinks on shiny black trays. Strawberry margaritas were in fashion, and although there wasn't a fresh strawberry to be seen growing in all of New York, each bulbous frosty glass had a fat red one perched upon its edge.

As if my notice had attracted it, I was confronted by one of the squatty little machines. I refused the drink offered and told it to go away, but the robot continued to entreat me to take a margarita, select something else from its list, or choose from its chestful of legal drugs. I knew that ignoring the metallic, bleating voice would not stop its insistence.

Robots always kept a record of each guest's orders or lack thereof. I was almost forced to choose a beverage to avoid drawing attention to myself, but the robot left when the snapping of fingers alerted it to another's need. I watched as it rolled away and then stopped to open its chest for the man's perusal.

An "adult" stereodrama started up, flashing colors and rippling water scenes on the ceiling in beat to "The Crooning Locusts." Various sexual acts were blended into the water scenes in an attempt to entice the crowd to a heightened interest in relationships. All at once, the room was too loud for me, and the crowd of people reminded me of restless, frightened sheep in a too-small corral.

I pushed my way towards the outer wall, needing air and quiet and hoping to look out over New York from so high up. Five men individually propositioned me on the way to my destination. The first one explained that the backrooms grew busy quickly and that the appointment time must be scheduled early, or there would be no party sex for him that night. All he needed, he assured me, was a female's name for the roster. When I attempted to go beyond him, he blocked my way and informed me that permission to use my name would not be a formal agreement to meet him at that appointed time. Perhaps he told the truth because the four who followed pitched the same kind of desperate plea. I told each of them that I didn't ever want my name listed on such a schedule, but each of the men's faces registered such disbelief I'm sure they thought I was just searching for a better prospect.

I'd almost made it to the outer wall when one of the robots caught up with me again. The smells of perfume and strawberries and the cooked mushrooms and peppers lying on skewers on the shiny black tray of the robot repulsed me. I was starting to feel desperate about reaching the window, hoping that it would contain some kind of balcony where I could get out of the room and breathe untainted air. Yet the robot kept thrusting its limp, dead-looking delicacies at me, demanding that I choose one and/or a drink.

"Diet cola," I ordered so it would leave me alone.

One of the robot's multiple hands held a platter over to the side. With another hand, it retrieved a tall, thin goblet from the inner cavity of its left side. It pushed the glass against its right side, and I heard the ping, ping of ice dropping down. A third hand discharged my cola into the glass.

"Diet cola," it said in its toneless, genderless voice, and it positioned the glass to what was, for me, about shoulder high. Reluctantly, I reached out, took the soda, and watched as the robot rolled away.

"Excellent things, these robots, yes?" said a deep male voice from behind me. I turned to look at him. He was a small man, only slightly taller than I was. I liked that, and I liked the color of the soft brown eyes that met mine. No, not brown, more like amber or the resin that you slide over violin strings.

"I'm not used to robots yet, I guess," I told him.

He nodded. His eyes slid over my body, but not rudely, and they returned to gaze into mine. "My name is Estevan. What is your name?"

Estevan was sipping a margarita. He took another swallow, waiting. I eyed the strawberry on the edge of his goblet, wondering if it was as sweet as the summer ones we sometimes green housed on the farm.

"Kira," I told him as he pulled the strawberry off the goblet's rim and then popped it into his mouth.

"A pretty name. You are booked?"

"No, and I don't choose to be," I said and started to push my way past him.

"Wait, Kira. I have respect that you do not wish this yet. Please, to talk awhile."

I didn't turn around, but I stopped to hear him out.

"I am not from here, Kira. I speak English not well yet. Perhaps I say the booking wrong."

"Where are you from?" I asked, turning to study his suit. The creamy velvet of the pants and jacket were stylish but a bit conventional for parties like this one. I liked the way the suit looked on him. It was much better than the orange toga I'd seen on the first guy.

"I am from Spain," he told me.

Estevan was probably very nice. Why did I have to be so choosy? "I'm new to all this, too," I said, taking a quick sip of my cola. I stared down at my glass, noticing all the little bubbles gathering around each ice cube, spewing little sparkles into the air. How could I ask my question without being rude? I took another gulp of soda and then just blurted it out. "In Spain, at a party like this, do you expect your women to . . . ?"

Estevan's eyes grew hard, and his cheeks clenched. "My women? From my family, they do not attend such parties." His anger had flared and gone.

"For you, this is new? This is the reason for which you say no?" He smiled from the corner of his mouth and then shrugged. "You are *muy bonita* — very pretty, Senorita Kira — *pero* I think you are similar with the women of my family. And for this purpose, I do not desire to instruct you. It is better that you go to your house."

I didn't want to go to the back room, but I sure didn't want to be told to go home, either.

"*Mi prima*, my little cousin, she has the eyes like yours with this fire inside. She does not like I say to go to the house. With her, what she thinks no is *muy importante*. I take her to the house, and I tell my aunt. With you is not possible." He shrugged his shoulders. "*Pero, no es bueno para ti.* Sorry. It is not good for you. Go home, pretty Kira. Go home," he said, as he moved away.

I was sorry to see him go, even if he had spent most of his time lecturing me. His accent had been so romantic. I could have listened all night. And his eyes had been really dreamy, with thick, full eyelashes and those gorgeous amber eyes. I sighed and shifted the drink in my hand. The napkin underneath was saturated by the outer moisture of the glass. I looked around for a place to put the glass down.

If I just set it on the floor, someone would probably tip it over onto the snowy, white carpeting, and I didn't want to be responsible for that. I held onto it until I passed one of the robots. While the server was busy handing out drinks to another party guest, I plunked down the glass, covered it with my wet napkin, and headed towards the outer window.

I'd been right — there probably was a balcony. The window frame was constructed to resemble (or be) a massive doorway. Like the entryway, it was made of genuine wood or a very expensive plastic reproduction that felt and smelled like fresh wood shavings. Even the doorknobs were elaborately constructed of the same material. I twisted and pulled at them, but they were well-locked.

A robot server came barreling towards me. "It is forbidden. It is forbidden. It is forbidden," it said.

I dropped my hand and stepped back. Robots don't feel emotions, but that one sure sounded stressed out. It edged toward me. I took another step backward. It rolled into the place I'd been standing, turned about and faced me, and continued droning, "It is forbidden. It is forbidden. It is forbidden."

"All right," I said. I threw up my hands as if it were a policeman robot with a gun at my chest. Its eyes still flashed an angry red, but it stopped repeating the warning. I backed away further until I'd allowed a group of guests to come between the robot and me, and then I continued watching, curious as to whether the owner of the suite would arrive to check the alarm. No one rushed over, nor did anyone pay the robot the slightest attention. After a minute, its eyes returned to green, and then, when nobody else threatened to open the door, it slowly rolled away.

What was probably a breathtaking view of the city had been turned into a video scene. The Swiss Alps was currently showing. It was so realistic an image I almost shivered. The snow was falling only lightly, but you could tell from the tiny spears of ice hanging from each pine-needled fir that the air was chilled outside. You could imagine your breath making little dragon puffs in the air. Heavy black clouds had formed a dark covering around the far-off peaks. They disappeared as it darkened.

What had been a twilight scene, seconds later, became the first rays of the morning sun. It streaked the sky with the soft, pale rose of dawn. Reds and oranges followed and as the light grew brighter, I saw that the snow was thawing, and the look of winter was gone. Tiny streamlets of melted snow gave way to green, and tiny blades of grass poked upwards. Lupines sent up spiny, velvet leaves, which opened outward, revealing dainty violet and lavender blooms. When the snow had all disappeared and grass the color of new maple leaves covered all the lower parts of the mountains, I turned to leave.

I found Cathy entwined with a lawyer I'd met at the first party. He nodded in recognition. I was surprised he remembered me. He was telling Cathy about his recent court case; I wondered if it was a new one or the same one he'd shared with me. He stopped talking as I approached.

"Did you visit the back yet?" Cathy wanted to know. "The rooms are just divine, and Carl and I learned so much about each other there." She gave his body a squeeze, then leaned her head against his shoulder.

I shook my head, trying not to see the sudden, knowing smile on Carl's face and the look in his eyes. Was he remembering how horrified I'd been when he'd made that suggestion to me?

"I'm ready to leave now," I told Cathy. "I'll catch a taxi and see you later, OK?

"Oh, Kira. You hardly gave the party a chance!" she scolded.

"I tried. I'm just not ready for this," I said.

"If you'd only just give it a chance," she pouted adorably, or at least Carl thought so. He gave Cathy's lip a pat and made a kissing sound with his lips.

"Let it be, Cathy. Kira'd be happier milking cows," Carl told her, laughing softly.

I don't know why I let him bother me. I couldn't help responding. "Probably would be more fun," I said. "I've never milked a cow before."

One thing I could say about Cathy's choice of men — this one had a great laugh. He was also observant. When he finished chuckling, he noticed that Cathy was getting a little irritated by his attention to me. He pulled her about, planted a sweet kiss on her lips, and said, "Don't get jealous, my dear. Kira and I know each other from a former party, and I see she hasn't changed any. She's still country old-fashioned."

Cathy dimpled up at him, and her teeth flashed him one of her breath-taking smiles. "You're so right, Carl. Kira's my roommate, and I can't do a thing about her. She just won't enjoy life!"

Perhaps the two of them were happy in this conversation, but I was beyond fidgeting. I cleared my throat to draw their eyes back to me and said, "All right! You two can discuss me to your heart's content, but I'm going home."

"To the farm?" Carl asked, smiling again.

His toothy grin wasn't half-bad. I suffered a sudden, very intense stab of jealousy for Cathy's backroom visit. "See you later," I told her and without another word to Carl, I turned on my heel and started to move away.

A sudden hand on my shoulder reeled me backward around to face him.

"I thought that was against the rules," I yelped, stunned that he'd touched me without permission.

Carl laughed. "Sexual encounters have rules, but brotherly assistance is strictly allowed."

Cathy wasn't saying anything. She was as shocked as I was. Any physical force, especially on one of the opposite gender, was grounds for expulsion from a party.

Carl ignored the look on her face and on mine and wagged his finger at me. "If you promise to listen, I'll let you go."

I shot a glance at Cathy, but she wasn't meeting my eyes. I couldn't tell what she was thinking about her new boyfriend. "I'm listening," I said.

As promised, he released me. Then he flung both of his hands up in the air and said, "Your honor, I plead a moment's insanity. Kira reminded me so much of my little sister that I forgot myself and grabbed her shoulder. I know that is an offense punishable by sixty days in jail, hard labor, and a diet of bread and water, but I plead for the court's mercy. What do you say, Judge Kira?"

Cathy was shooting out sparks from the corner of her eyes, and they were aimed at me. I knew I'd better leave, or our friendship was finished.

"Forgiven," I said, dropping my eyes and wondering if I dared turn and walk away.

"Good," Carl said and once more pulled Cathy into his arms. "Now, sweet Cathy, didn't you tell me that your car was here in the garage? And haven't we decided to fly up to Vermont and ski for the rest of the weekend?" He paused to kiss Cathy soundly on the lips before continuing. "Would it not then be logical to send Kira home in that car, my sweetness?"

Cathy was smiling again. She pulled down Carl's head and gave him one dynamite kiss while I stood there feeling like a fool. Finally, they surfaced. "I think Kira's still waiting for the key, Cathy," he said.

My roommate dug down in her purse and pulled up the emergency spare. "Here," she said, tossing it at me.

I caught it (and the wink that Carl gave me). I didn't check to see whether Cathy had noticed. I departed without looking back.

That night, in the apartment, I kept trying not to think about Carl and Cathy. But I kept seeing their lips joining and the way they'd melded into each other's bodies. Were they already on their way to Vermont? Were they laughing together and talking? Were they visiting some other back room where . . .?

Sleep was welcome that night. No alien monsters visited. Somehow, I almost missed them. At least they'd been company for me in my lonely dreams.

Chapter Four: Definition of Alien, *Unlike*

I cleaned the apartment, processed my clothes, and ordered groceries for the week. Yet, the weekend still dragged. On Sunday, after spending several hours in the bookstore, I bought a new book. That was one of the most pleasant parts of being in the city — the way you could spend all day poring over books, drinking coffee, eating a sandwich, and no one cared. No one booted you out or made you feel guilty for not buying anything. It felt wrong to loiter aimlessly, and the book I ended up with was one I could have found at the library, but it made a satisfying read late Sunday afternoon and into the night.

I was eager, though, for work to start again and thankful that for the next month, I had no more two-day weekends. On Monday, I rushed to the office, barricaded myself in my room, and made the connection with Cegan. My captain sounded almost as stressed as I was by the silence of the past two days.

It made me remember that he couldn't go to a party or to a bookstore. What was it like out there in space, with nothing to do, no places to go, and no way to relieve the boredom of being ship-bound?

Cegan and I quickly resumed our long conversations that the weekend had interrupted. We talked about space travel, hobbies, government, and everything else that came into our minds. It was so wonderful to have someone to tell everything to, and to hear his comments, and to argue and banter.

During the nights, I planned questions to ask him, and I thought up more things I wanted to tell him. And, although I continued to eat lunch with my friends, shop in the same stores, and giggle over silly movies with Cathy when she wasn't out with Carl, my life idled like a car in neutral. I stopped thinking about the wisdom of what I was doing, preferring to stay in a kind of twilight area where nothing was black or white — the non-thinking zone, I guess you'd call it.

The talks between the captain and me grew longer and longer. My work began to suffer. How could I schedule everything and maintain my connections with the other captains if I was always on the system with Cegan? I told Cegan that I could only talk with him first thing in the morning before I started work and at quitting time when we could relax and chat.

We spent many lovely hours laughing and exploring each other's lives and ideas. It was all but perfect, except that my friends began to question me about why I didn't leave with them anymore. They missed me, they said, and why was I no longer willing to go to the show with them when their dates fell through, or we had one of our "ladies only" outings? I came up with excuses for everything. My friends called me a workaholic and an apple polisher, but they couldn't entice me away from Cegan.

In my apartment, I heard the same kind of nagging from Cathy. Why wasn't I dating? Why wouldn't I go to another party? Why did I have to be difficult and different? How could I tell them that the parties, the dates, and all of their friendships paled beside Cegan? Cegan who listened, Cegan who spoke like a poet with words that held the treasures of a universe, Cegan who loved me.

As the weeks continued and their fussing failed to change my behavior, my friends eventually stopped badgering me. Then, I was even more consumed with Cegan, connected to him by our conversations and our sharings. Slowly, all the other ties that had once anchored me to a network of friends were severed. I didn't care. It was too late.

At fifteen days from Earth, although I'd never confessed my love, Cegan asked me to marry him. My heart soared, and I wanted to cry out, "Yes, of course I'll marry you," but I couldn't. The rainbow that every girl hopes for was my torture.

Once more, Cegan told me of his love, and I turned away. Even worse, on hearing his marriage proposal, I burst into tears.

I was devastated and hysterical; I even forgot to cut off the transline. How could I have been so cruel? Cegan was there at the other end, listening, and I didn't know it. I didn't realize. He let me cry it out, and only after I was wiping up the tears and sniveling like a schoolgirl did he begin to speak.

"I am sorry, my Kira. Have I hurt you unknowingly? How can I ease your pain?"

"It's not your fault, Cegan," I blubbered, losing my control again.

"Kira, my love," he kept saying over and over until I stopped to listen. "I am powerless to help you from this distance," he told me, and I knew his voice so well that I could hear the strain and picture the tears I suspected were in his eyes. "This is an agony for me, my dearest Kira. I should be holding you now. Perhaps you would allow me to touch my lips to your brow. I would not let one single tear of yours go uncomforted."

What would Cegan be holding me with? Did he have arms like ours, with skin, bones, and muscle? Were they warm arms that flowed with blood? Would they reach around me or be so strong they'd crush me in their grasp? Would his lips fill me with delight? Or would I close my eyes and shudder in revulsion?

My tears dried up. I felt guilty. Why hadn't I imagined it would come to this? Why hadn't I thought about it? Wasn't it the logical outcome between a male and a female? I knew that Natharans married.

When Cegan had said he loved me, shouldn't I have thought about where this was going?

But marriage to an alien — that couldn't be legal or moral. Would there be sex? And children? No, that could never be possible. How could I even think about marrying him? What would my father say?

My Natharan was still waiting as I let my mind flop about like a landed fish. "Oh, Cegan, I'm the one who's sorry," I said. "I'm so ashamed. What you said was honorable. It was a compliment to me. I shouldn't be crying. It's unforgivable. It's just that it's so hard for me to say 'no.'

You do understand that, don't you, Cegan? I love you, but I'm all mixed up inside. You know so many things, Cegan. So you must know that we can't marry. We're different species from different worlds! You do see that it can't work, don't you?"

"That we are from different worlds is irrelevant. Where is the law that says that two individuals must have been born on the same planet to share their thoughts or lives? I have given you my love, and you say that you feel this bond between us. Where, then, is the problem?"

"The problem is that Terrans don't marry aliens! You guys come to visit us, and then you leave, but there's no . . . "

"There is no reason that a Terran cannot. Natharan has many intermarriages between worlds. Most outer worlds do not find the co-mingling of species as abhorrent as you Terrans seem to."

"I don't find it abhorrent, Cegan, not exactly. But . . . I don't think it's legal."

"I have studied your laws, Kira. There are no international or national laws that prohibit such a marriage. In fact, those of your own country seem to encourage the possibility. There are several statutes banning segregation and discrimination, including those between Mars', Venus,' and our moons' inhabitants."

"Those are laws about Terrans who live off-world. They don't even mention aliens."

A long, drawn out, almost-human sigh told me that Cegan was as frustrated as I was, but when he continued, his voice was still calm with no hint of annoyance. "I love you, Kira. You are the soulmate I have longed for, the friend and partner I have sought. Nothing else matters. I ask you to connect your life to mine as an equal, as my wife, and in so doing, I promise to abide by and welcome whatever legal or social customs you wish to recognize, as long as they do not conflict with mine. And we will discuss each and every one of those differences until you no longer suffer the fear and anxiety I feel in you now."

"I'm not afraid of you, Cegan."

"Of course not, but your nightmares are of little green men, aren't they? You have been taught to fear me, Kira. I understand, and it was never my intent to frighten you with my need to be bonded with you. However, all relationships intensify in their depth, Kira, or they fall apart."

"Can't we just go on as we are, Cegan?"

Once more, he sighed so very humanly. How could a sound convey so much sadness, so much loneliness?

"For a while, my siren. We can continue for a while as we are . . . but if you trust me and believe that I will never hurt you, and if you love me as genuinely as you say, can you not see me as the one who loves you and forget our differences? Is my love for you and yours for me not more important than all the obstacles you place between us?"

"I want it to be, Cegan, but I don't know if I can think like that."

We talked of other things during the days that followed, yet every subject seemed to work its way back to marriage and commitment. Why was it so important to Cegan to have my promise that I would marry him? Why did I feel so much pressure from him about it? Didn't most men want to run the other way from matrimony?

I tried to explain to Cegan what marriage meant to a Terran woman. I thought it possible that his concept of "wedded bliss" might be something entirely different from Earth's. What did a Natharan really mean by marriage?

Cegan didn't ridicule my explanation or my questions. "You are right," he said. "For a while, we will need to confirm our understanding. Words that are assumed to have similar meanings at times do have shadings that vary in their use. Well thought, my dear.

"I would say that marriage on Natharan has the equivalent value as in your country. A Natharan marriage is a legal and moral joining that provides for children and for property. It creates a partnership for business and social development. The bonds between a married couple on Natharan are deep and binding, and your word 'divorce' has no translation in our language."

"What if couples fall out of love?"

"That is not possible. By your definition and ours, love can only deepen and thus grow greater."

"I wish that were true here," I said. "Those Natharans who married outsiders . . . "

"Outworlders, Kira. That is what we call them. But when one marries a Natharan, one is automatically a Natharan."

"Even if you are alien?"

"Only Natharans live on Natharan, Kira."

"OK, Cegan. I understand. But when a Natharan marries someone who wasn't once a Natharan, they can't have children, can they?"

"Yes, Kira, they can. There are many such children on Natharan, born from such intermarriages. You and I can have children. Is that your question?"

"You mean like in a test tube, right?"

"There are several options, Kira. We will not discuss that now."

"Isn't it important to discuss it if we are going to talk about marriage?"

"I will not discuss Natharan technology with you, Kira — not at this time. However, if it is our sexual compatibility that you are asking about, I can assure you that there is no problem. We are physically very complementary, my siren. No surgery would be required to make our physical unions enjoyable."

I gasped. "You would do surgery if . . ."

"It is not necessary, Kira," Cegan kept repeating over and over until I would listen again. Then he continued. "We are compatible, wonderfully compatible, my siren. Do you understand?"

"Cegan, this is crazy. I don't care what they do on Natharan. I can't . . ."

"Kira, Kira! Listen to me," he urged. "I have two arms that I long to encircle you with. I have lips that I wish I could spread warm kisses across your nose and cheeks. Do you not understand, Kira? I am a male who desires your body, but our marriage will only be as physical as you wish. Should you not feel the same desire for me that I feel for you, then our bond would only be of the soul. For I want to share my life with you on any level that you are capable of.

"I will take your hand in mine and show you the sunsets of other stars than yours. I will lead you to mountain peaks that challenge clouds of pink vapor and oceans whose waters glitter in a myriad of colors. I want to join my life to yours in sons and daughters. As I told you, we have the technology for that, Kira. Whether there is a physical bonding between us or not, there can be children from our union. You have only to open up your heart to trust, my Kira.

"You have said you do not fear me. Is that true, my dearest? If I have earned your trust that much, then how can you fear our marriage?

Don't you know that I will allow no harm to touch your spirit or your body? I will give you the freedom you crave and yet offer the guidance of a loving partner. I will value your dreams and encourage your imagination. I will honor you above all others. When you say 'yes' to me, my siren, your desires will be mine forever."

I couldn't speak. It sounded wonderful, but Cegan was asking too much of me.

For seven days, we didn't once discuss marriage, and although I couldn't sleep at night from debating with myself and worrying about it, the pressure I'd been feeling lessened. Then, it was, like it had been before, the usual chitchat of friends, the debates about philosophy and life in general, and the free exchanges about our days and our dreams.

But, too quickly, the pressure came back, and it was as if Cegan ignored my distress. The need I'd heard in his voice leaped out again. It came in the middle of a discussion we were having about education. I'd just told Cegan how I was thinking about attending the university and earning a degree, but I couldn't make up my mind about what I wanted to major in.

Cegan interrupted with an intensity that surprised me. "Kira, I have asked you to marry me. I want to take you with me to see worlds you have never been to. I want you to be my mate, to have children with me, to be at my side, my partner in the business. How can you be thinking of making a commitment to a program in an Earth university?"

"But I'm not sure I'm ready for marriage, and I can't think seriously about it until after we've met. When you land, we can go on a couple of dates, and . .."

"No. You don't understand. Kira. You must marry me before I land. Once I set foot on your planet, it will be too late for us. If you are not my bride at that moment, there can be no further words between us, forever."

Cegan's words panicked me. His plea was the sales pitch from a dishonest car dealer. "Sign the contract; don't check the engine."

"Why, Cegan?" I cried out. "Why does it have to be like that? Why can't we decide *after* you arrive on Earth?"

Was that a sigh I heard? No, it was more like the humming of a one-pitched note. It was minutes before Cegan spoke again, and then his voice was lower, calmer than before. "Kira," he said, "your love is fragile. I am aware of that. But this is a Natharan law. A bride and groom cannot meet face-to-face until they are wedded. I cannot break that code, even for you."

"But I'm not Natharan, Cegan," I argued. "Can't you do it the Terran way? We talk, we meet, we kiss?"

"No." The finality in Cegan's voice was jarring. "I want you in my life, at my side, with me always, but I am Natharan, and I must follow Natharan laws. If you cannot do that, then I will not see you when I arrive nor speak with you, and I will never have you as my wife. That is not arguable, Kira — no matter how much I love you."

There was such sadness in Cegan's voice that I felt like weeping. I wanted to soothe his hurt, to run my hand through his golden hair across his wrinkled brow. I wanted desperately to give in and say, "Yes, I'll marry you."

"Remember," Cegan continued, "I have never seen you either, my siren, but I know your soul, and because of that, I love you beyond all thought. I hope that will be enough for you, my love, but my ship is only seven days away now. I am not allowed by your government to circle in orbit nor to stop and wait, so you may have more time. You know as well as I the restrictions and regulations on outer world ships. Therefore, my dear, my siren, you must choose — for both of us or in seven more days, it will be too late forever."

"Yes" was almost on my tongue. But then the unfairness of his words slapped me back into sanity.

"Wait a minute, Cegan! A Natharan bride may not have seen her husband, but she knows what he more or less looks like. She knows the number of fingers on his hand and whether . . ." I stopped then, realizing that I'd almost said, "She knows whether he has a face like a fish." I couldn't say that to Cegan.

"Kira, if I told you I had nine fingers on each hand, would it change how we feel?"

"Oh, Cegan. I don't know. No, it's not just the number of fingers you have. Do you have nine?"

"No, Kira. Nor do I have claws or fang teeth to tear into your flesh. Is that what frightens you?"

I wanted to trust Cegan. I wanted to believe that two aliens could marry, but I couldn't say yes.

Inside my office, I was pacing back and forth. I glanced up at the clock. It was already 8:30 at night. We'd been talking for hours. It wasn't safe for me to stay this late. All the offices had closed, and the transtel-programmers had gone home long ago.

63

At this hour, only the robot cleaning crew would be about. The parking garage would be empty, too, except for the occasional vagrants who busted in. They were often users of harmful drugs like "Nirvana" or "Trance." I shivered, thinking about entering that tomb-like building where such drug heavies might be lingering.

"Cegan, I have to go home. It's late. Please, can we talk about this tomorrow?"

"In a moment, siren. I will give you words to sleep on, to dream, on perhaps," and, as if he knew exactly what I was thinking, Cegan made it even harder for me.

"I have already told you everything I can. My feelings are as open as a stellar map. But have you thought, my Kira, of what it would be like for you *without* our talks?"

The tears I'd sworn not to shed anymore flooded my eyes. I stared at the ceiling and watched the panels turn to lake water. "Stop it," I cried out.

"Kira, I swore I would never hurt you, and I know my words carry the sting of truth, but if I do not say them now, if I cannot win you over, the grief it causes both of us will be worn every day for the rest of our lives. I love you, Kira — without hesitation, without reservation, without having seen you," he said. "Can you not do the same?"

I forgot then about leaving the building. My anger flared. "You have seen pictures, Cegan. You know what a Terran looks like. What if you hadn't? What if I had fangs and a nose like an elephant? What if I breathed fire or dripped slime from my mouth?"

"I have been to many planets, Kira. I have not seen beings of intelligence with any of those lovely characteristics you have so vividly imagined. There is much more similarity between species than

64

you give credit to. Yet, I would marry you, Kira, if you slimed me or if your nose were distorted. I might not kiss you as eagerly with the threat of being burned by your mouth. Would the fangs be snake-like or carnivorous?"

"You're mocking me."

"No, my dearest. I love you." Then came one of those long silences that Cegan used to sift through his words and thoughts for explanations. "Kira, I will offer you this. We Natharans have come in contact with a few Terrans, and although your species is plagued by its fears of anything different, those Terrans who have seen us have not been repelled by our bodies. Does that help you, my soul's desire?"

I couldn't be silent then. What Cegan looked like was very important, but the problem was more than that. I wanted so much for him to understand. "Cegan, I do love you. But you don't know what it's like here. If a Terran trusts blindly, he ends up dead. How can I trust someone I've never met? I won't even go on a date with a man that a friend doesn't know. Can't you understand? I want to believe in you, Cegan, but I'd be a fool to."

Again, one of Cegan's silences followed my words. My office door wasn't adequately shut. I could hear the sound of a vacuum approaching from down the hall. Somewhere, the loud playing of a radio bumped and thumped with its cyber beat. Why would a cleaner robot be playing music?

"I am trying to understand, Kira," Cegan told me. "I hear the fear in your voice, and I know that trust is hard when there is fear. But if you cannot feel this bond between us, what proof can I offer you that will ease your fear and allow you to love my soul as I love yours?"

I couldn't respond. I didn't know the answer to that question. Cegan didn't seem to expect me to. He wished me pleasant dreams, then disconnected.

A cleaning robot was in the hall. It moved over to let me pass. "Good morning," it told me, even though it must be as dark as the depths of a well outside the Transtel System Building. Didn't the robot know "goodnight"?

The music I'd heard grew louder as I approached the elevator. A human was doing repairs on the elevator. It was the music I'd heard from my office.

"Mighty late, aren't you?" the man asked as he slammed the control panel shut. He reached over and pushed the elevator's door button for me.

"I had some things to finish up," I said. Was that what I'd been doing? Had I been "finishing up" the best part of my life?

When the elevator opened, the man waved me inside and then stepped in behind me. "It isn't safe here this late, young miss," he told me.

My heart pounded, and I moved further back, away from the man. I stared up at the digits, concentrating with all my force on those shifting numerals as we continued downward.

"I got a daughter just your age," the man said. "You don't have to be scared of me. I wouldn't hurt a flea — trust me."

Trust me! The words flung themselves right at my stomach. They echoed, "Trust me, trust me," all about the small metal box of an elevator. I cringed backwards against the heavy metal wall.

The elevator finally reached the floor of the garage. I stared at the huge door as it slowly slid open. I wanted to dart out, push into the man, hit him with my purse, and dash away, but my legs were frozen. I couldn't move away from the safety of the metal wall against my back. The door stood open. The man calmly stepped out. He stood at the side of it and turned to face me, his hand keeping the door from closing. "Aren't you coming?" he asked.

My legs were shaking, but the indignant look on his face at my lack of trust set my legs in motion. I scurried out and past him, half-walking, half-running to my car. I touched the door, hearing the click of the unlock and the sliding opening of the driver's-side door. I collapsed onto the seat, ordering "lock-on."

The car obeyed, and I heard the click of safety, but my voice was suddenly so scratchy from my fear that I had to give the order for my destination twice before the engine started. I heaved a wool blanket from the backseat and then covered up. My skin was icy cold, and I was shaking.

The car drove slowly in its journey toward the underground garage exit. As it took me by the elevator, I saw the man still standing there, watching over me. I waved to him. I hoped he could read my lips as they mouthed "Thank you."

When I arrived home, I found that I was alone again. I threw my purse onto one of the kitchen chairs and walked into my room. The light in my room was too bright. I turned it off and stared at my ceiling of stars. Where was Cegan now? Why was the silence of night so much emptier and so frightening when you were all alone?

"Trust me," Cegan kept repeating. That was the red flag of warning to a Terran, but my heart ached from the pain of his parting words. Never to talk with him again? Never to finally meet?

I reentered the living room and ordered the news on. I didn't want to hear it that night, but I needed the sound of a voice. Four different channels were talking about a wave of violence that was rampaging the subways. "Off," I ordered.

The resulting silence seemed almost as threatening. I walked over to the bookcase and chose a book. The one I picked had a cover with a woman gazing into the eyes of her boyfriend. He held out a diamond ring.

Cegan had told me that he'd reached the age of marriage, and if he returned to Natharan without a wife, a council would choose a group of women who were especially suitable for him. He and the women would talk without meeting, and then the selection would be made. Is that what I wanted? To send Cegan off to his alien bride?

"The council would be disappointed if I married you," I'd told Cegan half-jokingly. "It would rob them of their job."

"They wouldn't object, Kira," my captain had said, with that soft, deep voice of his that sent waves of pleasure through me. "We traders are encouraged to select a wife from other species. It is the Natharan plan for universal peace. With other species in our midst, our people learn not to fear the unknown."

For some reason, I became angry and snapped at him. "So that's why you want to marry me — because it will make your government happy?"

For a long time, Cegan had not spoken. I'd thought he'd disconnected, disgusted at last with my silliness, but the transline had indicated that the link was still open. Finally, unable to endure the silence any longer, I cried out that I was sorry.

"No, Kira," he responded immediately. "I was not upset by your words. I was simply pondering them. We Natharans grow silent when we struggle to comprehend a puzzling behavior."

I'd started to argue about whose fault it was, but Cegan had cut me off. "Listen, Kira, and allow me to explain.

"I will not always understand you, my siren, nor will you understand me. I believe that is not only true between alien cultures, but also between individuals of the same species. It is the wonder and the value of reaching out to communicate beyond one's self."

His words were beautiful. Tears formed in my eyes. I'd been forced to wipe them before I could respond. Somehow, I'd lost my chance to speak, and Cegan continued.

"Kira, forgive me if I have read you incorrectly, but are you saying that you value yourself so little you would believe in a falseness between us?"

His words hurt. I'd rushed to explain how hard it was to trust people. I'd talked all around Cegan's question. But when I was done, we both knew my answer. We Terrans do allow others to name our value. Perhaps that's why we have so many doubts, and why we cannot trust.

I shook the memories of that conversation from my head and opened up the book in my hand, the one with the eager lovers. I began to read. The woman married the guy on the cover, and he turned out to be a complete jerk. Then, she died mysteriously. Had her husband killed her?

My feet paced me back and forth. The carpet was heavily padded and soft, but I wished for the hard, untended paths around the farm where I'd grown up. There, I would have found rocks and twigs. I needed so badly to kick a rock, to break a twig into tiny little pieces, to scuff the dirt, or to chuck a rock into the little creek on the farm.

Carol Ann, the woman in the book, believed in her husband. Yet, she doubted him, too. Had her doubt caused her death, or was it her lack of belief in herself that was the cause? Shouldn't she have listened to the voice inside her that said her husband was not to be trusted?

"The Truth is always in you," Cegan kept instructing me. "When you are quiet and listen, the Truth will be known."

"But emotions interfere with good judgment!" I argued.

"That is true, Kira. Anger does intrude on wisdom, but mainly, your emotions are a reflection of your Rational Mind. They sort through all the facts and impressions you are not consciously aware of and analyze them. You Terrans speak of flashes of insight or the tapping of some alternate force, but your insight comes from that Rational Mind."

I remember laughing and saying, "My Rational Mind tells me that I have no business talking with an alien, especially one who professes to be in love with me."

But Cegan, as usual, had been ready with a quick rebuttal. "Not at all, my dear. Your Rational Mind can find no reason not to love me. It is only your Subconscious Mind that allows fear to confuse you."

"Subconscious, Rational, I can't tell the difference," I'd told him, bursting once more into the kind of nervous laughter that usually displayed frustration.

Cegan enjoyed such talks. I could somehow always sense when he was smiling. He'd smiled then. The warmth of it had filtered through my pores and spread inside me.

"And if the fear gets all mixed up with the truth, Cegan, how do I know what is really the truth? How can I tell then, what is the Rational and what is the Subconscious?"

I'd felt that same smile swelling into each word as he'd answered me, not as if he were laughing at me, but as if arguing such points or explaining them to me were the highlight of his day.

"My siren," he'd said in a tone that was such a caress it made me feel cherished and special. I'd had to swallow hard and force my mind to pay attention to his words rather than the sweet feelings his voice engendered in me. "You already know what Truth is."

I'd shaken my head in disagreement, but by the time I realized that, of course, he couldn't see me and had begun to gather the words for my argument, Cegan began to clarify it for me.

"The Truth does not make you doubt yourself, Kira."

I'd been numbed by the sweetness of my contentment and the warm coziness that Cegan's love brought me. I had hardly been able to appreciate the significance of his words. As was typical of him, somehow he'd understood that, and with his usual patience, he'd waited, not pressing on but allowing his words to take shape, to entwine themselves within my thoughts.

"The Truth does not make you doubt yourself." Had that been Carol Ann's mistake? Had she doubted herself and her own abilities? Was that what I was doing?

I sat down and flipped through the pages of the book. When I found the place I'd left off, I continued reading. It was a good mystery, so, of course, the villain was not the one the author intended you to suspect. The husband was not a jerk. It was Carol Ann's sister who'd been lying all the time. It was she who'd murdered Carol Ann.

So much for reading all the clues correctly! Where had my Rational Mind been when I'd analyzed and determined who the bad guy was? I didn't know until the very last page when the author finally told us. Was that an indication of my inability to judge Truth? That night, I spent another sleep of dreams wrestling with night demons and my doubts.

The next day at work, I set up an appointment with a Cedtarant space captain and the New York Manager of Trade. I entered the time and date into the computer band and was about to disconnect when the Cedtarant captain flashed back on.

"You are Kira?" he asked.

I hadn't given him my name. I was known on the circuit only by my number. Yet I answered him in the affirmative.

"You are the one in contact with the Natharan?" he continued.

How did this captain know that? What should I say? The light was still on. I knew he was waiting.

"Yes."

"This is good. We Cedtarants approve of your decision."

"My decision to do what?"

"Cegan has chosen wisely."

"I don't understand."

"Goodbye, Kira."

"Wait, I don't understand what you're telling me."

"We can tell you nothing."

"But what decision do you approve of?"

"You are young. That is good."

"Please, I don't understand."

"It is wise to be adaptable, young Kira."

"Did Cegan ask you to talk with me?"

"He would not like it. We Cedtarants cannot interfere."

"What do you mean, interfere?"

"Goodbye, Kira."

Of course, I immediately called Cegan. I was confused and scared. Why had the Cedtarant captain called me? How had he known my name?

Cegan demanded to know exactly what the Cedtarant had said. His order came in a voice of command that Cegan had never used with me before.

"I do not accept orders well," I told him curtly.

Instantly, the sunshine was back. I could feel the broadness of Cegan's smile as he said, "The acuity of your ear delights me, Kira. It is an ability that most space traders must develop. As I had surmised, you will make an excellent partner in the business. And you are correct, my dear. I permitted my irritation at the Cedtarant to influence my tone of voice with you. That was inexcusable. Forgive me. Nevertheless, it is very important for me to know exactly what the Cedtarant captain said to you."

I accepted Cegan's apology and repeated the conversation as best I could, but Cegan kept asking me about the precise wording, the tone of voice, and the pauses of silence. I couldn't remember all that.

"An individual's word choice is a clue to his intent, Kira. It is very important to analyze every word of a conversation. Even the spacing between words is to be noted."

"I am not a tape recorder," I snapped.

Cegan went into one of his silences. I closed my eyes and tried to make sense of the Cedtarant's call and, more importantly of Cegan's reaction.

"Ah, Kira," he said when he began to speak, his voice once again gentle. "I am sure the Cedtarant meant no harm. And your recall of the conversation does not matter. We will practice your skills later. There will be much time onboard the ship when we journey between systems."

"I am a Terran, Cegan. Perhaps I don't have the abilities you think I have."

"No, you have excellent potential, my siren. You have already demonstrated greater aptitude than the average Natharan apprentice."

That was interesting, but somehow, we'd gotten away from the crux of the matter. Why had the Cedtarant called me? I asked my question again.

"He should not have done so, Kira, and I shall make sure that none of the other captains contact you."

"Wait a minute! That sounds like a threat. I didn't mean to get him in trouble. I just didn't understand why he called me. Besides, if you're nonviolent, why do you use that tone? And come to think of it, why do all the others fear you if Natharans are really pacifists?"

"Kira, I will never hurt you."

"You're not answering me."

The whistled inhale sounded Cegan's dislike of the conversation. Because of this, I was also pretty sure that Cegan would evade my questions. Maybe he'd tell me again how he couldn't give out Natharan secrets, but I knew I couldn't trust Cegan if he couldn't be honest about this. It was that important to me! Once more, the silence stretched longer than I was comfortable with, and I fidgeted with my frustration.

"Kira," he said at last. "The bond between us is so strong now that I can feel the wall you are putting up between us. I have no choice but to answer you, yet it is difficult without your understanding of the whole, and that I cannot give you until the time is right. I know that to tell you to trust me will not soften your resolution, but I ask that you do so, or all is lost."

My fingers pounded the desk in irritation. "You're right, Cegan. That isn't enough anymore. You ask for my trust, but you don't trust *me*, and all this mystery makes you seem really untrustworthy."

Again, he whistled his dislike, but he continued without any of the long pauses of before. "Cedtarants are friendly, Kira. You have nothing to fear from them but the excess of their enthusiasm. They make the worst traders, yet it pleasures them to try, so they continue to barter their goods. Cedtarants especially like you Terrans, but that is not what you want to know, is it?"

Cegan began to hum. I'd thought he used that sound to make me listen, but he already had my full attention. I tried to wait for his song to end, but the notes of it seemed so jumbled that I couldn't find a pattern. Each time I thought I'd caught it, it changed, and I was forced to start again. "Cegan, you're driving me crazy with your humming!" I told him. "Can't you just answer me?"

"I am not finished with the words."

"Just tell me. Forget the spaces and the phrases, and just say it!"

"That is a very Terran thing that you ask. As I said, we will learn from each other." He sighed then, and I could not tell if it was from exasperation or just to clear his mind.

"It is difficult because there are no words for what we Natharans do. You said that the others fear us. The others do not fear Natharan. We do not fight them. We negotiate, Kira. In that, there is power. Others respect that. Can you understand? I realize that power in this way is not a concept of your culture."

"You mean you talk your way out of things?"

"And into."

"But we do that, too."

"Yes."

"But how could you make everyone afraid to discuss Natharan or to call me again?"

Again, Cegan whistled an inhale. I waited, hoping he wouldn't start humming again.

"Kira, no Terran knows as much of Natharan as you. Is that not enough?"

"You know everything about us. We don't hide from you. You're the one who is full of secrets, yet you keep telling me to trust. Why won't you just answer me, Cegan? You know that I've given you my promise not to tell anyone."

"You are a strong negotiator, Kira, but you treat Natharan as a riddle to be solved. I think it is more like your mythical Camelot, shrouded in the mists. I have given you the opportunity to join us and see if the answers you seek are there. You know how to get in."

"You're still dodging."

"But I have already told you, Kira, the others are not afraid of Natharan. We harbor no wish to bring harm to any species."

I was up and pacing. Cegan's answers were only making me angrier. "Evasions are lies," I said through my gritted teeth.

"All right, Kira. It is true that I have chosen you as my bondmate. How can I not give you what you need?

"But you must mention Natharan to no one — not your father or Frances or Cathy. No one understand? And it is not for Natharan's sake that you must promise this. Nothing I could tell you of Natharan would cause my world to harm you. The danger comes from your humankind. And I cannot protect you from them while I am so far away.

"I have explained to you in so many ways, my inquisitive bondmate, but you still do not see that the mystery of Natharan is merely a shield. We have no hostile weapons, Kira, although we have an armory of defensive ones.

"The mystery surrounding us began long before your civilization commenced. It originated because we did not wish to flaunt our advances in front of those who were technologically behind us. So, discussing our technology with outworlders was forbidden by law.

"But where there is one secret, the complexities build rivers of deception. Thus, concealment in all things concerning Natharan became the rule. Now, each little detail of Natharan is protected by thousands of years of silence, and every Natharan pledges to continue it.

Even what I have told you would be enough to strip me of my trader's license . . . unless you honor me by becoming my wife. For if we are bonded, then you will be Natharan, Kira, and our history and all the understandings of our culture will be yours."

I wondered if Cegan knew what blackmail was. I didn't stop to ask. "So everyone is afraid of you because they don't know what you'd do to them, and the truth is that you'd do nothing?"

"I did not say that, Kira. Natharan would retaliate, just not as you might imagine it."

"Wait a minute. You said that you didn't have aggressive weapons. How could you retaliate?"

"The power is in trade. A violent, confrontational species would no longer be permitted in the Grid. That would be a punishment they would find undesirable."

"And they couldn't hurt you anyway, right?"

"Are all Terrans as inquisitive as you?"

I ignored his teasing. "We really are different, Cegan. You Natharans have developed a culture of secrecy, which would be absolutely impossible for Terrans. As a species, we're horrible about keeping secrets! Yet I did give you my promise, and I mean it — that I'll never speak of any of this. Thank you for trusting me. I won't let you down."

It was difficult to concentrate on my work the rest of that day. I kept thinking about Cegan and all the things he'd told me. I reached up and tore down the photo of my dad I'd taped to the wall. I held it in my hands and studied it. What would my father think about Natharan and the things I'd been told?

I guess I knew what he'd say. He'd tell me to leave the city and come home. There were no secrets on a farm, he'd tell me. A man disked and planted and cared for the soil, and what he put into it, he always got out.

Yet there were secrets there, too. They were just short-winded ones. Tina's father ran off with Peter's mother. You couldn't tell that from looking at their places. Everyone pitched in and helped, and the crops on those two farms were just as good as anyone else's. But I guess the point was that even though it was a secret, everyone knew about it because secrets never last in the country.

But Cegan's world was a whole planet full of secrets, with devices I'd never heard of or seen, miraculous inventions and discoveries — anything you could imagine, Cegan told me, anything you desired. Wouldn't it be exciting to visit there?

Secrets weren't bad when you were part of them. And Natharans would welcome me to their land of Camelot, Cegan promised. Yet, would they really? Would I feel like I was part of the secrets, or would I forever be an Outworlder, even if they called me a Natharan?

I was staring at the picture in my hands, yet all I was seeing were the mists of Natharan. I refocused my eyes on the photo. My father was standing under the twisted oak that was in our backyard. It was a beautiful tree, with huge branches slanting askew at broken angles. I'd fallen from that tree once when I was little. It had frightened me badly, and I'd never climbed it again, but I'd often played under its shady limbs and rested against its scratchy, gray trunk.

I'd held tea parties for my dolls and watched fluffy, fat gray squirrels dart after acorns cradled in their fallen leaves. And, in the autumn, I'd laughingly smash those orange-red leaves underneath my feet just to hear the delightful, crunchy sound of it.

How I yearned for that tree right now. I missed the smell of it, the maple-like sweetness of its moist, decaying leaves, and the comfort of my hidden nest there under its arm-like branches, my cushioned, leafy seat, and the firmness of the solid trunk against my back.

Homesickness. That's what it was. I missed the simplicity of the farm and being with my dad. The oak tree receded, and the eyes of my father still stared at me. "Come home," the eyes were saying. But what would my father say if he knew about Cegan? I shuddered at the thought.

An almost empty water bottle sat on my desk. I picked it up. Then, I tilted it to drain the last few drops. I paused to study the now-emptied container. Why had I never realized how much like a baby's bottle it was? When had I stopped drinking from glasses?

I picked up the bottle and glared at its sports-top nipple. Was I a baby, needing to go home so Dad could make my decisions again? Angrily, I threw the bottle against the wall on my right and stuck the photo back up on the wall.

"Kira, are you all right?" Cegan was suddenly asking me. Had I opened the transystem to him without thinking? I hadn't meant to call him.

"Are you all right?" he asked again.

"Yes — no, I don't know. I'm just confused about everything, Cegan. It's all so complicated, isn't it? I was thinking about secrets and home and whether Natharan would accept me, and then I started remembering about the janitor who was trying to help me. My instincts told me he was dangerous, yet I found out that he was just a nice old man.

And, later, when I thought I knew who the murderer in a book I was reading was, I found out I was wrong. And my brain keeps doing flip-flops. I want to marry you, and then I . . . The truth is that I really can't recognize truth from falsehood, and most of the time, what you tell me is totally over my head!"

Cegan was silent a moment. I found myself staring down at my desk blotter. I'd drawn horses everywhere across it. Some were galloping, and some were grazing in green pastures. Several were jumping over obstacles, logs, and steeplechase jumps. My eyes picked at them critically, noting all the faults in my sketches. I was not an artist. A neck here and there was arched incorrectly, a leg was awkwardly placed, and one horse looked like a cartoon character with his bloated belly and overly rounded jaw.

I glanced over at the transystem, still surprised that it was on. Didn't I remember turning it off when we'd stopped talking about Natharan and said our goodbyes? I picked up a pencil and began reshaping the jaw of the cartoon horse.

"'Over my head' must have other meanings," Cegan said at last. "Can you say that in a different way, Kira?"

"It means I really don't understand you," I said. "Not when you're talking about Rational Mind and Subconscious or recognizing truth and falsehoods."

"I thought it must mean that. Your voice is full of frustration." He made a noise half-sigh, half-bark.

I smiled. The sound was so unlike Cegan.

"That was the call of the Senth," he explained. "They believe enlightenment can occur instantaneously if that call is done just right. What is most interesting, Kira, is that without enlightenment, the call can never be done correctly."

"Oh," I said, stumbling over the plastic bottle I'd thrown. I stopped and picked it up. "I still don't understand, Cegan. Even less now."

"Kira," Cegan said. His voice had softened even more. "You are very young." The velvety sound of his words was like a gentle stroking on my back. I wanted to protest, but I was strangely silent.

"A Terran rosebud does not open all at once. It takes hours, perhaps days, for the fullness to become apparent. Wisdom, likewise, is not born, my siren. It grows slowly, and we must be patient for its fullness."

I sighed. "That also doesn't explain anything."

There was another long silence. I sat back down and finished sketching a better jawbone for one horse, and then I worked on another's twisted leg. I had begun to think that Cegan was giving up on me. He was silent for so long.

I added a barn to my blotter and drew my father out in the garden with a hoe in his hand. Still, Cegan didn't speak. Twice, I checked the light of the transline. Then, I turned the blotter over and continued my drawings.

When Cegan finally started to talk, it startled me. But if he heard my indrawn breath of surprise, he didn't mention it. He'd obviously been thinking out his words, and he was so intent on their delivery that he didn't wish to stop. I put my pencil down and concentrated on listening.

"It is your fear that makes you doubt yourself, Kira. That is how you can recognize it. When Fear says that you are not able to swim across a small river, it has made you doubt that you can do it. Yet, your Rational Mind says, I have gone that far before, so there is no logic to my fear."

"But maybe the river has currents in the middle," I argued.

Cegan was not bothered by my interruption. I think his smile broadened. The words that followed held almost a hint of laughter if such a thing were possible for a Natharan.

"Maybe it is safest to stay in bed and not set foot out into the world. I hear there are sirens who lure you to their side yet offer no promises."

"That is unfair!"

"True," he admitted, and I swear his smile must have been full of teeth. It sounded so good-humored as he added, "Kira, all rivers have currents in the middle."

That night, as I lay in my bed, I knew I wouldn't be able to sleep. Not even the cocoa I'd drunk a few minutes before had relaxed me. But I stayed there, wishing I could visit with Cegan, wishing I could do more. What would it be like to talk with him with his arms around me? Would looking in his eyes give me the serenity that his words always did? Would there be more? Would I want him to . . .

I stopped my brain from tumbling endlessly over all my doubts. My eyes studied the room's ceiling, which was covered with little plastic stars glowing in the dark. They had been Cathy's present to me when I'd moved in. She'd teased me about being a farm girl, saying that I needed to see stars at night so I wouldn't feel homesick for the country.

Sometimes, the stars did remind me of home. There, you could look up and see a blackness so solid it was like black velvet, dark and rich. There was a smell of nighttime in the country, too. You'd breathe in deeply, and you could smell space, the cleanness and clearness of it.

Long ago, I'd visited a cave. I don't remember where it was, but I recall that three steps forward into its mouth stole all the summer heat. We tourists had shivered at the cold, but we'd walked forward and turned to the right. That was the start of the state's largest cavern, our guide informed us. He warned us to be careful of a huge hanging stalactite, and then, with his flashlight, he spotlighted a beautiful, crystallized lava-like formation of cool pastels and shimmering sparkles.

It was the part that came next still which still quickens my heart. The guide turned off his light, and the cold, hollow emptiness of the unexplored cavern made itself known. A dark descended on us then, a dark so black that my hand didn't show, and the people beside me seemed to sink into the dirt-covered floor. And I was alone.

It was only a moment, yet I'll never forget the smell or the taste of it. I thought it was only the dampness, the musty smell of wet, dripping rock, or perhaps the chemicals in the rock that had constructed all the formations, but it wasn't. It was the smell of the night black sky and the taste of the lonely emptiness that spread across the stars.

There is no taste or smell of the city at night. It doesn't get good and black. And when the sky should be clear and open, the stars don't even show. All the lights and noise of the night keep everyone from noticing, or maybe they just don't remember what the night sky should be like. Perhaps they never entered a cavern and dispelled the light, so they have no understanding of infinity.

I bet most city dwellers have never known the freedom of finding the right spot to call out into the night just to hear your voice echo over and over into the dark, deep, endlessness of it. I learned that, too, in the cavern with the night sky.

When I lived at home, I used to walk in the fields, away from the house and my parents. And when the stars came out, like new baby kittens opening their eyes for the first time, the stars would be staring down at me, and I'd be wishing I could go up there and wondering what it would be like.

Sometimes, I used to find myself wishing harder than I'd ever wished for anything else, pretending I could reach up and they would pull me towards them. Many times, I held my arms upward as long as

I could, closing my eyes so hard the blackness seemed like it was part of me, thinking perhaps that wishes came easier if you clenched your eyes until they hurt.

I'd known when I did it that nothing would ever happen, so I don't know why I kept on doing it. I just knew that the night sky filled me with such a painful longing that I had to keep trying to reach it. And, then, when my arms grew too tired to hold up any longer, I'd call out to the emptiness of it and wonder how far the echoes would go into the eternity of that night sky.

In an office elevator one day, I heard someone talking about how they got claustrophobia in elevators. I wanted to turn around and tell them how much I understood their panic. I felt that same desperation, wanting out yet but being trapped by air and gravity.

I spent all those years looking up at the sky, yearning to reach up and touch those winking stars, fighting off my own kind of claustrophobia. And I could go up there now. I could finally break free from my global prison and travel into the bosom of the sky. All I had to do was marry Cegan.

So why did I hesitate? Was Cegan right that I was no longer trapped by air and gravity but only by fear?

Could Cegan see those same stars from where he was? But what if his eyes didn't see them in the same way mine did? What if when we met, we didn't feel the same way about stars or planets or anything? What if . . .

The night was long. Worms of worry writhed inside my mind. I'd fall asleep, and then I'd wake to stare again at the stars on my ceiling. Again and again, I'd find myself wondering if Cegan was staring at the stars with the same anxiousness. Did he worry as much as I did? Or did Cegan always know the answers? Could I live with someone who knew all the answers?

Chapter Five: Definition of Alien, *Someone From Another Race*

The next morning, when I woke up, the sky was gloomy. Black clouds, like smoke, hung down over the city. I tried to smile as I pulled on my jeans and a long-sleeved blue-and-gray-plaid blouse. I turned to look at myself in the mirror, twisting about to view my reflection on all sides.

My outfit didn't fit with the city. I threw on a v-necked sweater in the same color blue as the blouse. That was better, but I still looked too country. No matter, I wasn't taking off the jeans. I needed the feel of them on my body that morning. My hair was a mess; strands of curls were flying every which way. I smoothed them down, combing them with my fingers.

I stayed away from the boots I wanted to wear. I could just see Frances and the others laughing when I walked in. I wouldn't go that far to feel the way I used to. As I pulled on my socks, once more my eyes took in my reflection.

It was a good thing I had extra time. I would need it to work on my makeup. Dark smudges, like recovering bruises, underlined my eyes. The lack of sleep these past weeks had certainly not improved my looks. My eyes looked haunted, my skin pale. I looked like someone recovering from the flu.

Why wasn't I skipping about, singing a song, free and easy, as my dad would say? Shouldn't I feel that great lightness that comes from letting go of worry? I had made my decision. I loved Cegan, but lots of people loved people they couldn't marry. Lots of people walked away from situations they couldn't handle, and they went on to live wonderful lives, didn't they?

I'd had a great time with my pretend. I'd believed for a while that I was different, that I could attempt something no one else would dare. Visiting other planets journeying through space — those were silly, childhood fantasies, like pledging to love an alien. None of it was part of the real world. Why did my day feel so miserable?

The huge office clock was striking 7:00 as I walked into the building. All eyes riveted magnetically to me as if I were the North Pole. Why was everyone staring at me?

I walked forward slowly with that sense in the pit of my stomach that said, "I think I'm going to be fired." The feeling grew stronger as I approached my office. Mr. Dee was standing at the entrance.

Without a word, he waved me in and followed after, shutting the door behind us. I staggered to my desk and collapsed into my chair. Whatever my boss was going to say, I just wanted it to be over quickly.

Mr. Dee's eyes glowered at me. His foot was tapping at the carpet as if he'd like to find me there and squish me. I'd always thought he was such a gentleman, easy going, pleasant to work for. I felt sick.

"What's going on?" Mr. Dee roared.

A stray white hair on his shoulder ruined the sharp appearance of his black suit jacket. It matched perfectly with those in the few spots where his remaining hair still grew. The shadow where he'd shaved that morning seemed darker than usual.

I shrugged my shoulders and shook my head. I didn't trust my voice to speak. I had no idea what Mr. Dee was talking about. I'd never had a complaint. I'd never misguided anyone or goofed up an appointment. The only thing I had ever done . . . Cegan. My boss must have found out that I'd been talking with Cegan, but even that was not against any rules.

Mr. Dee studied my face. "You don't know what happened, do you?" His foot stopped its angry tapping. He pulled up a chair and sat down across from me.

Again, I shook my head. Maybe this wasn't about Cegan if Mr. Dee was asking me that.

My boss cleared his throat. It sounded like a car backing on gravel. I noticed that his tie was the same color as my sweater.

Last night, scores of pictures of Natharan started coming in over the system. Pictures of buildings, mountains, and the top one's a picture of a sunset," Mr. Dee said, pointing to my desk. A folder was sitting there. I opened it and saw that it was filled with Xeroxed photos, photos of a place I'd only heard of.

My hands shook so badly that I kept dropping the pages, but I couldn't stop sorting through them, hunting for what I wanted to see. I looked through every one of the pictures before I realized that not one photo showed a citizen of Natharan. I wanted to cry or to laugh. I did neither. I simply looked up at Mr. Dee and waited to hear what he would say.

His eyes were boring into mine. They were dark-brown eyes, like coffee beans or Hershey's kisses. His mouth had well-worn cracks about the sides. Did they always crinkle downwards? It made him look so sad.

The silence and his stare were rattling me badly. I looked again at the photo in my hand. Slabs of concrete were diagonally set into the sides of a rectangular building. Fern-like plants grew from the angles on all its sides, cascading down in overlapping greenery. On the roof, the same concrete slabs jutted upwards, making the roof look like a porcupine's back. A grass-like growth filled in the spaces between each slab. It was an unusual architecture, but not necessarily an alien-looking one.

In the background, the wide, flat grasslands that Cegan had told me of stretched far off into the distance. The photo could have been taken anywhere. Only the sky, with its slightly yellow cast and the twin suns off in the corner, gave the viewer the knowledge that it wasn't a Terran scene.

"I don't understand, Mr. Dee," I said. "I didn't ask for these." But was that the truth? Were these pictures meant to be Cegan's reassurance?

Mr. Dee moved from the uncomfortable guest's chair to sit on the corner of my desk. "Those pictures are interesting, Miss Stevens. I am sure that you could sell them for a great deal of money if Transtel Systems doesn't decide that it has the legal rights to them. But it is the letters that have brought my interest," he said, and his rather fat index finger pointed down to a box on the floor.

"Letters?" I repeated dully, following the direction of his point.

"Yes. This morning about 5:00 A.M., the letters started arriving, and they continued for an hour and thirty-six minutes, one after the other, in a continuous flow. No one could shut them off. The letters continued to print even on machines that were completely disconnected. Can you explain that one, Miss Stevens?"

I shook my head, but I was thinking about some of the times the transystem had been switched off when Cegan had begun to talk. What were the limits to Natharan technology?

Once more, the gravel rattled as Mr. Dee cleared his throat. Then he pulled out a wrinkled white linen handkerchief and blew heavily into its interior. When he was through, he shoved it back into his pocket and continued. "In those letters, there are recommendations and avowals from business connections across the known universe, letters from friends and relatives, and I don't know who else.

I think I saw two or three hundred of them, all about a Natharan space captain named Cegan. And they are all addressed to a Kira Stevens. Now, would you like to tell me what is going on? Not only the company, but I suspect our federal government and the Bureau of Alien Communications and Interrelations will want to know why an alien, one from a planet no one has even heard of, is contacting you."

Mr. Dee had crossed his arms and was waiting for my answer. He was my boss, and I knew I should be trembling because he would probably fire me and maybe even yell at me, but there was something about him at that moment that reminded me of my father. Mr. Dee didn't look like my dad. My boss was short, pudgy, and balding, but his eyes and the way he sat there, just like Dad would have, waiting for me to explain, were so familiar.

I ended up telling Mr. Dee all about Cegan. I was surprised when I finished that Mr. Dee didn't start yelling at me or dismissing me with a snap of his fingers. Instead, he seemed genuinely concerned, and like my dad, he seemed to care.

"Let me talk to this . . . captain," Mr. Dee demanded.

Without a word, I obeyed and punched in the numbers. Cegan came online immediately. "Kira, did you get the information? Does it make it easier for you?"

Mr. Dee stood up abruptly and waved me aside. Then he sat down in my chair and reached for the on-switch. "You are speaking with Mr. Albert Dee, Miss Steven's administrator and also the Senior Vice President of the New York Division of Transtel Systems International.

It appears, Captain, that you have been misusing company equipment. This will be reported to the Bureau for Alien Communications and Interrelations. May I suggest that your government may not be receptive to such a complaint?"

I wanted to pace back and forth, but I didn't dare. I tiptoed over to the visitor's chair and hesitantly sat down. I sincerely wished that I had not eaten that piece of half-burned toast I'd breakfasted on. I wished I were back in bed.

Cegan replied just as firmly. "I am a member of the United Trader's League, Mr. Dee. I do not believe that I have transgressed any of your laws."

I love you, Cegan, I wanted to whisper to him. Was it too late? I glanced again at the box of letters on the floor. All those people had vouched for Cegan. He was real, as real as Frances' Ivy, as real as Mr. Dee. I was wrong to think I could say "no" to him. I needed Cegan. I needed him in my life, no matter who he was or what he was.

Mr. Dee was switching back on. I almost mentioned that Cegan didn't need the on/off switch. I was pretty sure that he could listen or speak whenever he wanted. But I'd given my word that I wouldn't mention Natharan technology to anyone.

"I see," Mr. Dee replied coldly. He loosened the tie at his throat and leaned slightly forward. "As I said, Captain Cegan, this matter will be reported. However, there is another matter that has come to my attention. Miss Stevens is an employee of this firm, and as her superior I have a responsibility to protect her from people . . . uh, aliens like you."

Cegan tapped the response light. I could see the color change from my seat across the desk. Mr. Dee saw it, too, but he ignored it. Unless Cegan broke his own rule, he was forced to wait until Mr. Dee flipped the switch again.

"I'm turning off the recorder now, Captain, and I have scrambled the line, so there won't be any problems with recordings on your side, either. I want this little chat we're about to have to be off the record and just between you and me.

"I don't like what I've heard from Miss Stevens about your conduct, Captain . . ."

"He has been honorable . . ." I burst in.

"Sit down, Miss Stevens. Do I need to ask you to leave?"

I sat down and closed my mouth. Mr. Dee was definitely a lot like my father.

"You space captains, you think you can take anything you want. I've dealt with hundreds of you in my lifetime. I've seen you scoop up our jewels and historical artifacts as if they were just keepsakes for your visit. But a Terran woman is not a souvenir."

Angrily, Mr. Dee's finger slammed the switch to the on-position. It was only a second before Cegan was countering with the same coldly incensed voice.

"Mr. Dee, you are incorrect in several of your statements. I will ignore most of them because the only matter of significance is Kira Stevens. I intend for her to become my wife. If that is not sufficiently honorable in your eyes, perhaps you can remove yourself as our intermediary."

I gasped, and it drew Mr. Dee's attention. "Not very smart, is he?" Mr. Dee said to me. "Perhaps that is the answer," he said, drawing up his eyebrows until they resembled two miniature rain clouds on each side of his brow. "Do you have another way to communicate with this captain if I take you off the system?"

"No! Please don't do that to us! Cegan!"

"You know he can't hear you when the switch is off," Mr. Dee reminded me.

I didn't like the look on Mr. Dee's face as he thought about taking me off the transystem. I was just about to argue my case when Cegan started speaking again.

"I have allowed anger to rule wisdom," Cegan apologized. "I believe, Mr. Dee, that, in your way, you are demonstrating your concern for Kira's welfare. It is inappropriate of me to reject your assistance in that endeavor."

Mr. Dee picked up one of the photos that Cegan had sent and studied it. Then, he glanced over at me, sighed heavily, and flicked the switch off. "I was called in early this morning, Captain, to figure out what to do about this situation. I took a moment to research Natharan.

It only took a moment because there was almost no data about your planet in our registries. These photos and your contact are the first. It seems most unlikely that you would have volunteered them without supreme justification. I find that interesting.

"How old are you, Cegan?" Mr. Dee asked, flipping the switch.

"You are correct; the photos may be cause for a reprimand when I return to Natharan. However, if sending them to her wins Kira as my bride, I will deem whatever penalty justified. As to your other question, I have calculated my age to be approximately thirty of your years."

The switch was green for Mr. Dee to speak, but he just sat there in thought, his fingers sorting through the pictures.

"Mr. Dee, please . . ." I started.

"No, I am not finished with your captain. Sit down."

Mr. Dee's voice was no longer as angry. I began to hope.

"You have threatened my employee as if you were a small-town gangster, Captain, what with your ultimatums and your bullying."

I opened my mouth to protest that absurdity, but Mr. Dee's index finger was already warning me to be still.

"Miss Stevens has a perfect record here with us. She is young, far too young to be thinking about marriage to anyone! And, especially not to someone of your age. Of course, that's just my own opinion. The company does not take a stand about who should or should not be married."

I shifted uncomfortably in my chair.

"Miss Stevens is a bright girl. Never once has she snarled the lines or made a mess of her scheduling. I hope it won't be necessary to lose her because of your interference, Captain."

Mr. Dee sat there for a moment, gazing at me. His eyes were looking me over as if he'd just noticed me sitting there for the first time.

"And another thing, Captain, I've just noticed that my employee also happens to be quite pretty. That makes this business with you even harder to understand. If she were ugly as sin, I suppose there'd be some logic to it, but she's slender and . . ."

"Mr. Dee, Cegan doesn't need to hear . . ."

"He will hear what I want him to hear. Do sit down, or I'm going to have to jot a note in your file about insubordination."

Mr. Dee was being worse than my father. I couldn't stand much more of this.

"I don't know what your concept of beauty is, Captain," Mr. Dee continued. "It couldn't possibly be the same as ours, but by human standards, Miss Stevens is a very attractive person. She has blue eyes that sparkle, especially now when she's a little mad at me. She has good skin and long, curly hair. Wish I had some of your hair, young lady."

Why was he doing this? What was the point?

"Why, I suspect, if she wanted, Miss Stevens could get married like this," he said, snapping his fingers together.

I sighed heavily, but Mr. Dee ignored me and went right on talking to Cegan.

"Undoubtedly, she has a family that loves her." He turned in the chair and glanced at me. "Your parents are alive, aren't they?"

"My father is."

"See, she has a father, one who loves her very much, I bet. Captain, have you talked to the girl's father to see how he feels about an alien son-in-law? Where I come from, a girl never marries without her father's permission. I don't know how it is in your world, Captain, but here, what a father thinks still matters . . ."

"Mr. Dee," I interrupted again.

"What?" He spun around to glare at me.

"Please, none of this is necessary. Cegan didn't . . ."

"He didn't pressure you to marry him in . . . how many days, Captain?"

"Six Earth days," Cegan answered, almost too quickly for the usual Earth transit.

Mr. Dee didn't seem to notice. "You ought to be shot, putting that kind of pressure on this young girl. Why do you do this? Not that I understand how she could even contemplate marrying an alien. Why, Captain? What are you after?"

"It is our law," Cegan told him. "A Natharan couple must marry before meeting their intended. I do not wish to harm Kira in any way, but I must abide by Natharan law. I have tried to ease her worries with the pictures of my planet and with the letters from my business contacts and friends."

"I see. No, I don't see, but you aliens have your own way of doing things." Mr. Dee turned to look at me. "Kira, why? Why would you even think about . . . ?" He was shaking his head and gesturing with his palms up in the air. Every word was being emphasized with an upward jerk of his hands.

It was the same question I'd been asking myself for weeks. "I was going to say "no," Mr. Dee, and then all this came." I walked over to the desk and picked up the picture of a sunset on Natharan. The colors were so different. It was as if they had been filtered through yellows and greens. But the sky was beautiful. Desperately, I wanted to see that Natharan sunset with my own eyes.

"I don't know, but I think now I should say "yes." Why did my voice sound so weak? Why was I still stuck in this quicksand of indecision?

I lifted up the box of letters and let my fingers drift through the pile. Who were all these people who had written to me about Cegan? The letter on top was from a business associate of Cegan's, testifying that he had been a friend of my Natharan for eighteen of the past years. Another letter writer lavishly praised Cegan's honesty and integrity. I dug down and pulled out a letter from the middle of the box. It was from a Baskante who wrote to congratulate me on my choice of husband. I laughed out loud as I continued reading. The letter went on to say that a Natharan's only fault was that he or she was monogamous. The Baskante warned me that I would find monogamy boring, and he offered to allow me to join his household with his seventeen current wives.

Mr. Dee was watching me read the letters. "Kira, may I call you that?" he asked, waiting for my nod. "Perhaps this is none of my business, but I have a daughter only a little older than you. I would hate for someone to have allowed her to make such a decision without any fatherly advice. What do you really know about this space captain?"

Mr. Dee's eyes were kind. I could feel his concern. I closed my eyes and thought of Cegan, and our sometimes-heated discussions over Rational Mind and moral rights, the way he always teased me and made me laugh, the way Cegan had let me ride his words through the Natharan mists.

I opened my eyes and looked at Mr. Dee. His loosened tie had a gold tie clasp with a Celtic design on it. On the golden disk was what appeared to be a coiled snake attempting to bite its own tail. I pulled my eyes away and looked back down at the letters.

"I have only Cegan's words, Mr. Dee. Maybe that's not proof enough for you, but I know the way Cegan thinks and feels. I know who he is. I believe he's the kindest, most wonderful, most intelligent, and gentlest person I've ever known. And I know also, Mr. Dee, how I feel about Cegan. I love him. And if you or anyone else takes Cegan away from me, and I would never forgive you for that, I would be miserable every day of the rest of my life!"

"Here," Mr. Dee said, passing me the tissue box that had been sitting next to his arm.

I sponged my eyes, wiped my nose, and sniffled a couple of times. The room had suddenly become very quiet. I looked up to see that Mr. Dee's eyes were staring at me. At least, I thought, at first, they were.

But his eyes were fixed and glazed. A moment more, he quietly stared like that, and then he reached over and flipped the transystem back on. "You still there, Captain?"

Cegan acknowledged by flipping the switch back and forth.

"Why do you really want to marry a Terran?"

"I want to marry Kira."

Mr. Dee rotated the chair until his back was to me. There was a perfect bald circle on the crown of his head. It was as shiny as a polished apple. What did Cegan's gold hair look like?

Mr. Dee was gripping the desk fiercely. His knuckles were whitening. "Yes, but why exactly do you want to marry Kira?" he demanded, in attack mode.

Cegan whistled his frustration. "Why is it necessary to explain all this to you?" he asked. "Is Kira not an adult? Is she not free and capable of making her own decisions in this regard?"

Mr. Dee sat up straighter. I do not think he was used to being questioned when he demanded information. His hands clasped the desk even tighter. The veins on the back of his fists bulged like two purple rivers surging with the current.

"Captain," he said, "if you plan to continue using the transystem for this . . . this folly, you better start talking."

Cegan paused a moment. I knew he was searching for words in his usual manner. I fervently hoped that he wouldn't start humming. Instead, he whistled once, and when he began to verbalize his answer to Mr. Dee, the edge I'd heard in his voice, the indignation, was no longer there.

"Kira's voice," Cegan began, "even from the first, was as pleasing as a baby's smile. It brought me back to her, desirous to hear more, and every conversation after that tied me closer to her. Then, when she laughed that first time, it pierced my heart. Surely, you have known love like that, Mr. Dee. Reason plays no part when the heart swells with adoration.

"You say that Kira is beautiful, but you have told me only what you see. I can tell you of the beauty of her soul, a soul that has the truest qualities of nobility. In Natharan, we would say that Kira has 'the honesty of light', meaning she possesses all of life's blessings. She will be treasured in Natharan.

"You asked me why I wish to marry Kira. I ask you, Sir, who would not? In all the worlds I have visited, no blossom blooms as sweetly as Kira. She charms with her spontaneity and her gentle breath of innocence. Her mind delights me with its facility and its instinctive, astute perceptions. She challenges me, she makes me smile, and she makes life an enchantment.

I understand your hesitation in allowing me to have Kira as my wife. If she were mine, I would guard her equally, knowing that her loss would be the cessation of life's vitality and purpose. Can you not understand how this could be, Mr. Dee?"

Mr. Dee "harrumphed," but he didn't stop Cegan.

"I love Kira. She is the song that sings the melody within me. She is my sunlight, my rain, and the air I breathe. Allow Kira to be my wife, and I will offer her my love and my life forever."

I looked over at Mr. Dee. Surely, Cegan had won him over. I knew I couldn't say "no." I loved Cegan. And he was right. Nothing mattered beyond that.

But Mr. Dee was still frowning. "Perhaps you are a poet, Captain? I think you express yourself almost too well. But words are not so difficult to say. Sometimes, they are only the chaff on the wheat field. Do you understand the meaning of that, Captain?"

"Yes," Cegan answered after waiting for the on-switch.

"Where are the eatable kernels, Captain? How does Kira know that you will not beat her or kill her? How does she know that Natharan does not want her as a research subject? Grim concepts, Captain, but on Earth, we've seen them all."

Mr. Dee turned to look back at me, but he continued speaking to Cegan. "I do not know, Captain, why it is not Kira's father who is saying these things to you."

Mr. Dee stood up and began pacing back and forth across the room. Then, he turned to come back to me. "Have you even told your father about your alien captain, Kira? It is a father's right to know the person his daughter thinks she wants to marry."

I shook my head "no."

Mr. Dee pointed his index finger at me and shook it in my face. "To be young is to be foolish. Why do you never consult with your elders? Why do the young first make the mistakes and only then ask for our help to get them out of the messes they've made?"

Poor Mr. Dee. He was getting so worked up that I feared he'd have a heart attack. His face was red and puffy.

"My daughter is just like you," he continued. "She married a bum who will never rise in the business world, and now she says she wants a divorce!" Mr. Dee strode over to the transystem. "Are you still there, Captain?" he asked.

"Yes."

"Well, maybe there is merit in the Natharan way, communication with no physical contact, but only among one's own species, Captain. Surely, there is a girl somewhere who looks like you that you could love without taking one of ours."

"I have already answered that, Mr. Dee. I love Kira and only Kira."

"So you say, Captain, and maybe you do, but these letters on Kira's desk don't prove your honesty. You could have been the sender of them, Captain. Let Kira talk with someone who knows you, preferably a human. If he will testify that you are who you say you are and that you will treat Kira courteously, then perhaps she can make her decision more wisely. Until this witness to your integrity arrives, I refuse to allow Kira to talk on the transline. I won't have her misery on my conscience."

Mr. Dee switched off the transystem without waiting for Cegan's reply. Then, he turned to me. "You have misused company property, young lady. That is reason enough to fire you, but I won't do so if you promise to spend the day with your father and tell him what's been going on here."

I was stuck. I could do nothing but accept his condition. I just wished that he understood what he was asking. Dad would probably try to lock me in the basement until Cegan's ship arrived if I told him all the details.

Besides, I knew my father wasn't going to like anything about Cegan. It wouldn't have mattered if the captain had been a bank president or a Supreme Court judge. No man would ever please my father. I knew that for a fact because the whole time I had been in high school, Dad had put each one of my dates through "the Inquisition."

My friends used to joke about my dad having a torture chamber in the basement for any guy who fooled around with me. Thanks to him,

I was probably the only eighteen-year-old virgin in all of New York City! And I'd only just broken out of the prison cell to go live in an apartment, and now I needed to tell Dad about Cegan?

Now, please, don't get me wrong. My dad had been my warden all the years of my life, but part of the problem, and the reason I'd put up with it for so long, was that I loved my father. And warden or not, he was still the greatest dad anyone's ever had. I just couldn't see telling him about Cegan!

Chapter Six: Definition of Alien, *One Who Offers Allegiance to Another Country*

For once, there wasn't any traffic on the way to my dad's, and the weather was beautiful. My Autocar sailed through the kilometers just when I wanted it to slow down. I pulled off the turnpike an exit too early, deciding that taking the old highway would give me some time to figure out what I was going to say.

I decided to stop at a diner for some coffee. As I pulled off into the driveway, I groaned as gravel ping-ponged against my car. A neon sign was blinking a red-lettered "HELLO" as I ordered the door lock.

The breeze, as I stepped out, was cool, but I didn't bother with my coat. It felt good to get out of the car, and despite my lack of a jacket, I did a couple of toe stretches and breathed in deeply before sprinting to the diner's double door. Inside, an old radio was blaring computerized country. I recognized the song from my graduation year.

The stools held four or five customers, regulars, I imagined. They all turned to stare at me. I was surprised that I didn't recognize any of them, but I was still a county away from home.

"Good morning," I said as I walked up to the counter. I guess my voice hadn't picked up any of the city accents. They all turned back to their coffee after noting that I was one of them. I sat down on one of the shiny, fake leather stools and asked the waitress for a cup of coffee to go. When she poured it, I added some milk and sugar and pulled out a ten.

The waitress twisted her pencil into her artificially red-streaked hair and rang up my sale. "Aren't you the Stevens girl?" she asked through a wad of gum. Her lashes were caked with old-fashioned mascara in a shade of green I found particularly nauseous, especially with her ruby red lips.

When I nodded, she went on about how she knew my dad and had seen me ride in the local rodeos. "You're real good at those barrels! But I hear you cashed in your boots for city heels. Why do you want to do that?"

"Gotta try something different, I guess," I told her.

We exchanged smiles, and she gave me my change. Her smile got even bigger when I put down a two-dollar bill.

"Say hello to your dad," she called out as I went out the door.

The rest of the drive, I kept thinking about what I'd said to the waitress. "Gotta try something different." You couldn't get any more different than marrying an alien. But "different" wasn't what I was looking for.

I loved farming and living out in the country, yet I wanted more than I'd found in Roxanne. That's why I'd gone to New York. But how on Earth was I going to tell Dad that I'd found what I wanted, but he lived even farther away than the Big Apple?

I ordered the radio to search for a new air station. After a minute of static, it tuned into the one I used to listen to growing up. Flashing Dancer was crooning about broken promises and cast-off lies. I sang along with him and followed up with several oldies from The Dream Breakers.

It was good to be back on home turf, but fifteen minutes later, I ended up pulling into Dad's long, gravel driveway, still without a clue about how I was going to tell my father about Cegan. It was time to pray for a miracle!

I had brought the pictures of Natharan and the letters from his friends that he'd faxed to me, but I doubted that my dad would look at them. Dad wouldn't trust an alien to deliver the daily newspaper.

I arrived early enough for lunch. Dad fixed us meatloaf sandwiches that tasted a lot better than my usual yogurt and French fries. I nibbled at one of the pickling cucumbers and Dad was working his way through the rest of the radishes. It was pleasant, chatting companionably, sitting there at the old burnished oak kitchen table.

Muffin, our longhaired tabby, walked in, meowing for a lap, and I gave her one. Dad didn't like animals at the table much, but he sat back, shook his head at me, and didn't say a thing. He stretched out his long legs. I knew they pained him sometimes, and there was a moment of tenseness in his face that told me that today was one of those days.

"You OK, Dad?" I asked. "You want me to go get one of your pills?"

"Nah, I'm fine, Kira." He picked up his coffee mug and gulped from it. I could see the steam still rising when he put it down. It always surprised me that Dad could drink coffee when it was that hot.

"I'm glad you had the time for a visit, Kira. Didn't you have to work today?"

I pretended to be engrossed in smoothing down Muffin's fur. It was soft and nice to touch. I wished I could bury my face in it, lie there listening to her purr, and not have to think.

"Mr. Dee, my boss, told me I could have the day off," I explained. "I think he thought I looked tired or something."

"You do look tired, Kira, but I thought you worked in a big building with lots of people. How come this Mr. Dee was noticing how tired you look?"

"I don't know," I lied. "He just did. He's nice to everyone, Dad."

"This Mr. Dee, isn't he an older man?"

I could feel Dad studying me. His green eyes were keenly examining my face. He was like a bloodhound, sniffing for a trail. "Dad, you know he's your age. I told you that before. And no, there's nothing between us."

"Well, that's good. Coffee?" He was up pouring another mug full. I didn't know how a man his age could drink three or four pots of coffee every day and still be as calm as a cow chewing her cud on a lazy, sunny day.

"No thanks, Dad."

He sat back down, stretched out his long legs once more, ran a hand through his thinning, white hair, and said, "You gonna tell me what the problem is, or you gonna just sit there brooding on it for a while?"

There was no way to tell Dad gently. The word "male" raised his blood pressure. "I'm kind of thinking about getting married, Dad."

He smiled. "If you're only 'kind of thinking about it,' you aren't nearly ready to do anything about it," he told me.

"Dad, I love him. I really love him."

The smile disappeared, and the lines on my father's forehead became prominent again. "Now, that's a whole bunch different, Kira. Yet, you didn't come out and say that at first. I think you got more to tell."

I couldn't get any further. I'd used up all the neutral ground I could think of. Like a coward, I kept my eyes down on Muffin.

Dad shifted in his chair and then leaned forward. "Kira, you know if there's any problem, no matter what it is, I'll stand by you. You pregnant?"

I looked up, meeting his eyes fully. "No, Dad," I said, "It's nothing like that."

He let out his breath, shifted, and nodded. "That's good, Kira. I didn't think so, but I thought I'd better let you know how I feel in case something like that ever did come up. Those city boys don't always have the respect for a girl that they should."

He took another sip of his coffee. I could feel him searching around for the next problem. "You already know I think you're too young to be getting married. Girls nowadays are waiting until they're almost thirty. But I don't think you're asking for opinions here. What's this fellow do for a living, Kira?"

Space captain was not on the list of my dad's acceptable options. For the next ten minutes, Dad ranted about how dangerous space travel was and how "I could love a doctor just as well."

"I know, Dad," I said, "but I don't love a doctor."

Dad was doing some heavy thinking. "This guy must be a good bit older than you to be captain of a ship already. How old is he?"

"He's thirty."

"That's way too old for you!" Dad said, pouncing on it as triumphantly as a cat catching a floating feather. "Why, he's almost twice your age! Find yourself a nice young fellow, maybe twenty-one or two. A man of thirty years is ready to settle down and have children. You need some growing room first, Kira."

I sighed. It was worse than I had expected, and I hadn't even gotten to the difficult part. I studied the yellow daisies on the wallpaper. Their petals, yellow as sunshine, with their orange centers and green stems, were so cheerful. The daisies had been Mom's favorite wallpaper, so Dad and I just kept putting up the same pattern whenever the paper started looking faded.

"Dad, you're not listening. I love Cegan."

"That's his name? That's a funny name."

Wisely, I kept still.

"How much education does this man have?"

"I don't know, Dad, but he's widely read. He's a philosopher and almost a poet the way he uses words."

I could tell that my dad was not impressed. "Poets don't make money, and neither do philosophers. That man of yours would do better learning something useful. Why doesn't he go into engineering? That's a good field for a man of today." Dad got out his pipe and stuffed it into his mouth. I knew then he was just getting started with the questions.

Years ago, when Mom was alive, she'd asked Dad to stop smoking. Dad always acted like he wasn't listening, but he'd waited for Mom's birthday, wrapped up all his tobacco, and given it to her as a present. From that day, Dad never smoked again.

Even after Mom died, he didn't start up, but when he had heavy thinking to do, he got out the pipe and held it in his mouth, unlit, his lips twisting around the sides as his words floated out.

"I suppose you'll do as you want, Kira. You don't listen to me anymore," Dad said, laying down heavy guilt. "If you did, you'd never have left the farm to go live in that city. "When do I meet this fellow of yours?"

I couldn't even picture that. My hand was stroking Muffin, and a part of me was listening to her purr, but I think, more than anything, I was trying to draw in that peaceful feeling that cats have when they're all curled up and contented.

"He lands in six days," I told my dad.

I thought the worst was over then. Dad sat there rocking back and forth on the kitchen chair, punching the hole the chair made in the flooring a little bit deeper. Dad was examining me. I knew that look. I'd seen it too many times in high school when he smelled something slightly off, and he was determined to figure it out. He stood up, poured himself still another mug of coffee and stood towering over me. "You're hiding something, Kira. You going to tell me, or am I supposed to guess?"

I felt suddenly like I was going down for the third round. I couldn't meet Dad's eyes. How could I tell him? It was all so complicated.

Dad sat back down in his chair. I could smell his coffee. Why did the aroma of it always make me thirsty? I picked up Muffin and carried her with me to get a diet cola out of the refrigerator. When I returned, I repositioned the cat and opened my drink. Dad used the time to prepare for his next attack. "How long have you known this man, Kira?"

"Thirty days," I told him.

"Not long enough for a lifetime commitment, is it?" He took another sip of coffee and started to choke on it. I rose up, ready to pound him on the back, but he waved me back down.

It didn't slow him much. He was a hound on the scent, and I felt like the prey about to get treed.

"You mean the total time that you and this captain have been together is thirty days, and then he left, and now he's coming back?"

The silence that followed made Muffin's purr all the louder. "No, Cegan has never been to Earth," I said, proud of the way my voice sounded so calm and sure.

"Then you've never even met him? What kind of a relationship . . . Hold it, Kira." Dad's coffee leaped out of the cup and splashed onto the table. I passed him my napkin. "The pieces aren't coming together here, girl. This captain, he must be from a Terran outpost, right? Mars, Venus, the moon?"

I kept shaking my head with each suggestion. I don't know why I couldn't just blurt it all out. Dad wouldn't let it go until he had all the pieces. I was playing with a spoon, trying to keep from looking at my father. It flipped up in an arc, flew over the table, and fell onto the floor. The clink of it hitting the faded brown flooring was loud in the silence between us. Only the faint beat of the clock on the stove told me that the world was moving onward beyond the look in my father's eyes.

Dad dragged his chair over closer to mine. He sagged down into his chair like his spine had sat in vinegar too long. I couldn't keep my eyes from glancing at his face. I wish I hadn't. My father, the most alive man I'd ever seen, looked wilted as a summer crop when the water pressure was down.

All my life, I'd seen Dad with his muscles bulging through an old worn-out tee shirt advertising Morgan's Heifers or Peabody Seed Company, tossing huge bales of hay or sacks of grain. One of my friends had said he looked like the Marlboro Man, and the name stuck. But someone had let the air out of the Marlboro Man, and he was flattening as I watched.

"Dad, I'm sorry, but I love him. Don't you see? It doesn't matter. It's who he is inside. That's all that's important."

"Let me see if I understand this, Kira," Dad said in the voice of a condemned man resigned to his death. "The man you say you want to marry isn't an Earthman? He's one of those aliens with antennas or three arms?"

I didn't answer my father. My hands were squeezing at the empty soda can. It suddenly crunched together, leaving the sides all bent and distorted. One piece jutted upwards like a broken arm with the bone out of alignment. The noise of the can crushing in my hand sent Muffin fleeing with a meow of protest. I felt deserted.

Dad looked almost as bad as my can, like someone had shriveled him, prune-like, into an old man. "Oh, Kira, my little Kira," he kept saying as he stood up and wrapped his arms around me. "Thank God you've come home. We're not going to discuss this, Child. There's nothing to say, not now, while you're so worked up. We'll take a walk and go check on your horse."

I knew what Dad was saying. Everyone thought the same way. No one would ever understand. "It's what's inside that counts, not what a person looks like."

That's what everyone kept telling you until you believed it, and you chose 'nice", but then Mr. Nice didn't match up to their expectations. I'd heard it all in high school. "Well, he's nice, but couldn't you have done a little better in the looks department? I mean, you're pretty. Why would you settle for someone who's such a dog?"

I didn't bother saying any of that to Dad. I was just as guilty of the same kind of thoughts. I didn't know if I could accept Cegan, even though I loved him, but I knew I had to try. Even if Cegan appeared so awful to my Terran eyes that the sight of him revolted me, I would get used to him.

There were people with horrible scars or burns across the face, and they were still loved. How could I do less? I was going to marry Cegan, no matter what he looked like or what Dad or anyone said.

I stood up and walked outside with my father. We spoke no more of Cegan that afternoon, nor would we have, except for Thenus Sachem. He came by in response to Mr. Dee's challenge to Cegan.

Chapter Seven: Definition of Alien,
Adverse

Mr. Sachem was a retired Terran space captain. He told us that he was a friend of Cegan's, although I'd never heard Cegan mention him. But Mr. Dee had called my dad, and my dad and he had talked, and the result was that Mr. Sachem came for dinner.

Mr. Sachem was a great deal shorter than I'd imagined a space captain to be. And he was scrawny, too, scrawny as a newborn foal, as Dad would have put it. In fact, he wasn't anything at all like my image of what a captain should be like. His skin was pale and sallow, as if his health was poor. He had almost no muscles in his shoulders or upper arms, and his hands were so big and ungainly that it was hard to imagine him even handling the controls of a ship.

Only his eyes were acceptable. They were olive-green and sharply observant. I could tell in a single glance that he had the kind of eyes that would slice down into you and lay open your darkest secrets. If I'd had anything to hide, I'm sure that I would have been afraid of him. Mr. Sachem, I decided, should have been a private investigator. His eyes were better suited for ferreting out the truth than for working out spatial grid coordinates.

Right after the introductions, talk about the weather, and a discussion of Mr. Sachem's drive out to the farm, Dad started telling him one of his favorite stories, and the fine little lines of crinkled skin at the sides of Mr. Sachem's eyes that Dad always said were the evidence of good humor, grew deeper and deeper.

And when the end of the tale came, and it was the place where you were supposed to laugh, Mr. Sachem caught on, and he launched into a deep roar of a laugh. That was like sliding into home base with my dad. Unfortunately, Mr. Sachem didn't even look like a private investigator when he was horse-laughing. I wondered how well he and Cegan really knew each other.

I attempted to break into the conversation to ask about Cegan, but Dad more or less ordered me to the kitchen to "check on dinner." Dad and I had finished most of the preparation for the meal earlier when Mr. Dee first called. The roast was in the oven, and the potatoes and carrots were with it. I still had the biscuits to pop in at the last moment and gravy to make, but I didn't think it was appropriate for Dad and Mr. Sachem to have any conversations without me.

As I walked towards the kitchen, I heard Dad laughing and telling Mr. Sachem what a good cook I was and how he was in for a treat. Dad knew I wouldn't argue in front of the company, but I thought he was pushing it.

When I announced that it was time for dinner, Dad and Mr. Sachem took their places at the old oak table. Dad said grace, and then they dug in. Mr. Sachem seemed right at home. He passed on the cucumber and zucchini slaw and the homegrown tomato slices, juicy and red as ketchup, but he took second helpings of everything else.

When he sopped up the gravy from the roast with the last biscuit, my father beamed. Dad didn't hold with much talking while eating was going on. But when Mr. Sachem's plate was empty, the last bit of potato was on Dad's fork, and I had just refilled their mugs again with fresh, steaming coffee, I figured I'd given enough time for politeness.

"So you know Cegan," I started in. "Is he honorable?"

Mr. Sachem put down his coffee mug and looked me over. It was as if he hadn't really taken the time to size me up before, and he needed to classify me before answering my question. "Kira, if I may call you by your first name, young lady?"

I nodded, as much to urge him on as anything. I didn't care what he called me. I just wanted to hear what he'd come to say.

"How about that apple pie, Kira?" said my father.

"Dad!" I groaned, but one look at my father and I was up slicing the pie. Then, the men had to have ice cream on it and refills on the coffee. By the time I finally sat down again, they were both finishing their pie. I waited, not offering any second pieces.

Mr. Sachem slid back his chair, dropped his napkin onto the pie saucer, and once more looked me over. "Good supper, Kira. I thank you two for inviting me to it."

He took another sip of his coffee, and then he said, "All right, Kira. Yes, Cegan is an honorable man. I've never met a Natharan who wasn't. They won't lie even if it's to save their life, and you just about can't make them mad.

They won't fight either. They talk things out until you want to scream, or else they just walk away if talking doesn't work."

He glanced over at Dad and then continued. "I once saw Cegan's dad, Chinep, take a punch in the stomach. When Chinep got back up off the ground, darned if he didn't apologize to the man who'd hit him, saying that there must have been a problem in the communication of their transaction."

Mr. Sachem laughed then, a deep barrel of a laugh, a laugh that told us how much he savored the memory. "They're not cowards, though," he continued, turning to face my father. "I've seen a Natharan stand up to somebody twice his size. Have you ever seen a Pigaar? They're almost ten feet tall and look more like a tree than a person.

Well, I saw a Natharan stand up to one of them and dammed... Sorry, Kira," he said, pausing to glance my way. "I mean, darned if that Pigaar fellow didn't back down! Of course, it's a heck of a lot easier to be brave when you've got technology backing you up. Natharans have stuff we can't even begin to figure out. It seems like every time they have a need for something, they just go right out and invent it, like nobody ever told them that there aren't solutions for everything."

Mr. Sachem stopped then and swallowed the last few gulps of coffee in his cup. I got up and poured him some more. Where was he putting it?

"Thank you, Kira," he told me. "This sure is good coffee." He took another sip and continued, "Cegan and his father are, I guess you'd say, a level above the others; that is, as traders, they rank pretty high. The father's retired now. Chinep, that's Cegan's father, as I said, he figured, like me, that there's a time to quit spacing. He lives on Natharan, from what I hear. I've never been there. You gotta get invited, and not too many spacers are. Never been any Terrans there, to my knowledge."

Mr. Sachem reached over and helped himself to one of the apples in the centerpiece bowl. It was a New England Gold, picked fresh that morning. Mr. Sachem's slightly yellow teeth carved it up in less than a minute flat. He laid the core on his empty pie plate and continued.

"Cegan took over his father's business, and he does as well as his father did with it, which is saying a lot. The family's pretty well off, not hurting for money, anyway. Cegan's got a good brain. I guess that's causing him some trouble on Natharan.

They've been after him to mate and have some children. I've heard that Natharan leaves most of their citizens alone. They are free to be bachelors or old maids as long as they want unless somebody scores real high on the special tests. A high score means marriage by a certain date. Did Cegan tell you that his due date comes up the moment he returns to Natharan?"

I nodded.

Mr. Sachem barrel-laughed again. "Kind of funny that high score thing. It's like a penalty. Good sense in it, though. Here, big families have nothing to do with intelligence. Perhaps Earth should have some kind of screening like that."

Then, as if noticing that neither my dad nor I was interested in this tangent, Mr. Sachem sighed and got back on track.

"They say Natharan's real pretty. I wouldn't mind going to see it myself, Kira, but I wouldn't marry one of them to do so. Those Natharans aren't human, Kira. It just isn't worth it. Mr. Dee told me about how Cegan is pressuring you to marry him. I like Natharans, Kira, and I like Cegan, but I think you have to remember that they're different than we are."

"How? What do they look like?" I asked.

Mr. Sachem lifted up his hand to halt my speech. His eyes darkened, and he frowned at me. "You know fully well that I can't talk about Cegan's form or what Natharans as a species look like. It's some kind of wedding rule, or at least that's what Cegan says. I wouldn't know about that, but I am sworn to secrecy on their appearance, and that's a promise that I made long before I met Cegan or his father."

Dad was shifting in his chair. This was not what he needed to hear.

"I know about the Natharan's need for secrecy, but can't you tell us anything else?" I asked.

"I suppose I can tell you that at the first contact I made with them, I guess it would be about twenty, no, twenty-three years ago, they used some kind of machine on me. So no matter how you bat those sapphire eyes of yours, Kira, I can't talk any more freely about Natharans than I already have. That machine makes a humming noise in my ears if I try to talk about Natharans. Now Cegan gave me some kind of treatment that came over the transit, and he said that would help me a little, but that humming's starting up again, and it can get pretty nasty."

He reached into his pocket and took out a bottle of aspirin. His glass of water was still full, but he swallowed three pills with a big gulp of coffee.

I shot a glance over at my father. His complexion had paled as much as Mr. Sachem's. Dad must have felt my eyes on him, but he didn't look at me. He was staring at the trader.

Mr. Sachem caught my father's eyes. "Don't worry about it, Mr. Stevens. Natharans do not deal in pain. It was a suitable bargain for what trade with them brought me."

"Can it be undone?" my father was asking.

"Perhaps," he said, glancing at me. "If Cegan lands, our world will see what a Natharan looks like. Besides, from the things Cegan said, I think that Kira probably knows a great deal about Natharan, and according to Cegan, nothing is going to be imprinted on her brain, no matter what her decision is. So I would guess that if Kira is free to talk about Natharan, it wouldn't much matter if I did."

"Imprinted?" my dad and I said at the same time.

"It's a good thing that Cegan's family is high up there in the government. I don't think most of the traders I've had dealings with would have any control as to whether a Terran contact was imprinted or not."

All this was not giving Dad a good feeling about Natharan. I poured both of the men another round of coffee and started a new pot. I was glad to have something to do with my hands, but it didn't keep me from wishing that Cegan hadn't kept so many secrets from me.

When I sat back down, my father reached out his hand and seized mine. "Kira, you can't go through with this. Who knows what thcy'll do to you? They're not like us . . ."

I gently removed my hand from his. "Mr. Sachem has said nothing to change my mind, Dad. Natharan is not going to hurt me. Mr. Sachem just said that. And Cegan loves me, and I love him. Nothing else matters."

"Girl, are you blind?" Mrs. Sachem said. "Your father's right. It's true that the Natharans won't hurt you. I made Cegan give me his word on that before I'd even promise to come see you. Cegan wouldn't lie. You can be assured of that.

But you've been to SpacePort, Kira. You know what monstrosities are possible. I won't say that Natharans are nasty-looking, but I won't tell you that they're human, either, and I can't see why a sweet girl like you, pretty as a picture and young . . . why would you even consider an alien like that?"

Mr. Sachem looked over at my father and shook his head as if the whole thing puzzled him. His hands curled around the coffee mug and tightened their grip until the knuckles looked like white bones.

"Listen, girl," he said, speaking slowly, as if I were a child. "You've been on a farm all your life, so I'm going to take a chance that your father won't kick me out for talking like this in front of you, but it needs to be said, and you need to think about it. Have you ever seen a chicken try to mate with a lamb? Or a horse with a cow? Animals have more sense than humans. They know to stick to their own kind." Mr. Sachem slid back his chair and stood up. It was obvious he wanted to leave.

"Wait, please," I said. "Please let me ask you . . ."

Dad stood up, too. "You can't leave without another taste of Kira's apple pie, Mr. Sachem," Dad said as he walked towards the sink. Mr. Sachem glanced at the pie and sat back down.

"Do you think Cegan would ever hurt me?" I asked.

"You mean like physically?" Mr. Sachem said, pulling his eyes reluctantly away from the sight of Dad heaping vanilla ice cream on top of the piece of pie he'd just sliced.

"Nah. I told you none of them is violent. The hurting would only be inside you." Mr. Sachem's eyes met mine briefly and then went back to the large piece of pie that Dad was carrying towards him.

Dad plopped the pie down in front of Mr. Sachem and poured coffee into both cups.

"Thank you, Sir," our visitor said. Then he picked up his fork and pierced the pie right in the middle. He broke off a hunk and shoveled it eagerly into his mouth. "See, Kira," he said, in between chews, "if you lived there in Natharan, you'd start to realize that you could never be one of them cause you're a Terran, not a Natharan."

"Cegan wouldn't expect me to look like a Natharan," I said, not following where Mr. Sachem was headed.

"You ever hear the story of the Ugly Duckling, Kira?" he asked, but he didn't wait for me to reply. "It doesn't matter what you look like, girl. That story is not about being ugly. It's about being with your own kind, and if you aren't with people who look like you, you get pretty unhappy."

I sighed. Hearing his opinions about life wasn't what I wanted to talk about. "Mr. Sachem, can't you even hint about what Natharans look like? Would I scream if I saw them?"

Mr. Sachem finished up his pie, took a last swallow of coffee, and turned to my father. "I thank you kindly for the meal, Mr. Stevens. I wish to God your daughter would listen, but I can see it in her eyes. She's only heard the parts she wants to hear."

The two men clasped hands in a firm shake. I sighed and stared at the dishes. I'd be leaving in the morning, and I wanted to make sure everything was shiny and clean for Dad. I thanked Mr. Sachem for coming and gave him my goodbyes. Then, I rolled up my sleeves and set to work.

I set my alarm that night for 4:00 A.M. I'd decided to leave before Dad got up. It was the only way I figured I could get out of hearing more lectures. But it's hard to beat a farmer out of bed. Dad was already up the next morning, and the coffee was on.

We ate breakfast together and talked about Molly's new calf and whether it would be a good year for oat hay. When it was time to leave, I was still worrying about Dad making a scene, but all he said was, "I want to be there when that captain lands, Kira."

I promised I'd call and let him know. I didn't tell Dad it would be too late to stop it all, that I'd already be married to Cegan. How could I tell him there would be no church wedding, no long white dress, and no father at the altar giving me away?

I hugged my dad goodbye and then tried to pull away, but he held me close, refusing to let me back away. "How do you know, Kira, that you two can . . . ?"

I was embarrassed. It was good that Dad still held me in his bear grip. I couldn't have looked him in the eyes. "Cegan says our bodies are compatible in that way, Dad, and remember what Mr. Sachem said, 'Natharans don't lie.'"

"They can be wrong, though," said my father as he released me.

I was feeling guilt so strong I was almost ill from not telling Dad the whole truth. And it was doubly hard not to say anything because I really wanted Dad to be there. Yet, I just couldn't bear to have his doubts with me when I pledged myself to Cegan.

The drive back to the city was easy. I'd faced the worst. I was through with the indecision that had tormented my days. I drove directly to Transtel Systems and went to talk with Mr. Dee.

"Thank you for sending Mr. Sachem," I said.

"You're welcome, Kira. I checked him out for you first before I gave him your father's phone number. I'm glad he was able to straighten you out about that marrying an alien business."

I was staring at my hands. I'd never been that much of a nail biter, and I'd never held a cigarette, but I wished right then I had something to hold on to or something to do with my hands other than let them grip each other like two little lost children.

"Mr. Dee," I said. "I know your feelings about Cegan, and if you don't do this, it's OK, but I'd like to ask you to stand in proxy when I get married."

"Damn it, girl! I thought Mr. Sachem convinced you this wedding was absurd."

"Mr. Dee, I love Cegan, and he loves me. I want to marry him according to Natharan law. Will you help me, please?"

Mr. Dee did not wilt as my dad had. He only sighed and looked resigned. "What did your father say?"

"He wants to meet Cegan, but he knows he can't forbid me to do this. I am an adult, sir."

Mr. Dee studied me. I lifted up my eyes and met his look. I let him see that I had made my decision and I would stand by it.

"You're absolutely positive, Kira?"

I nodded my head and said, "I love Cegan. I'm positive that I want to marry him."

Mr. Dee groaned. His hands flew up in a gesture of exasperation. Then they fell, and he sighed heavily, his shoulders drooping, his eyes closing a moment before saying, "All right, Kira, I will help you. Not because I agree with your decision. I think you're wrong, very wrong, young lady. I think that humans should stick with humans.

"But it's your life, and you do have the right to choose how you'll live it. You'll have to sign a release for Transtel Systems, of course, and chances are the company will want to use your picture in future ads. It might be good publicity, I suppose. We'll have to see. If you'll agree to that . . .?"

Mr. Dee passed me the document to sign, and I was instructed to read it over thoroughly and to let him know when I was ready to sign so he could have my signature witnessed. He left me alone in the office, and I did the best that I could to interpret all the legal jargon. Mainly, it sounded like the company was making sure that I wouldn't sue them if I later found out that the marriage was a disaster.

That seemed only fair. There was another clause about using my name and picture for company promotions and infomercials. I didn't understand about that part at all. How could my picture ever benefit Transtel Systems?

A few minutes later, Mr. Cronick, an attorney for the New York office, came in and was introduced to me. He talked to me about the document I was about to sign, wanting to know that I understood it fully. Mr. Dee's secretary, Ms. Teeler, and Mr. Dee were my witnesses. Mr. Cronick put down his official stamp, and the document was rushed off for processing.

I thought then that I'd concluded the business portion of the marriage, but I still had other paperwork to fill out for the state of New York. The attorney helped me with those forms, and the company physician took my blood sample. Then Mr. Cronick called a minister he knew, and the big event was officially scheduled.

Later, there were those who found fault with Transtel System for pushing me into the marriage. The company truly didn't. It was only by my request that it went along with it.

Those same people also blamed Mr. Dee for turning the marriage into an advertising campaign, but it was Mr. Dee who argued with the attorney to delay the release of the news, and no matter what anyone says, I'll always be grateful for his assistance. Mr. Dee was a good friend to me, and he stood by me throughout everything that happened in the following week.

But I have moved forward in the story, and I must back up to where I was at that moment. I was still sitting in that same red vinyl chair in Mr. Dee's office. I was feeling numb, removed from the business all around me.

I found it so much easier to let the nice attorney and my boss take charge, and although I was appreciative of their efforts, I did feel a little dazed by how quickly the whole thing had escalated. It was as if, somehow, I'd lost control.

My finger kept tracing the arm seam on the chair. The seam curved downward into a graceful arch, like a heavy cord of strength against the smooth vinyl. In my memory, that seam is more vivid than the conversations occurring all around me, and later, when Cegan asked me about what the attorney and Mr. Dee had discussed, I was amazed that I couldn't remember more.

"Thank you, Mr. Dee. Thank you, Mr. Cronick" was all I heard myself saying at various strategic moments, and I remember stroking that seam over and over, wondering what Cegan was doing, and thinking that I should call him and let him know what was happening.

A sudden thought at one juncture finally broke me from my lethargy. I remembered how I wanted to ask Frances to come to my wedding.

"Mr. Dee . . ." I began.

"Yes, Kira, what is it?" Mr. Dee asked, staring curiously at my hand as it gripped the chair's arm.

"I just thought, sir, if it's all right with you, could I ask Frances to be a witness at the wedding?"

Mr. Dee smiled. He seemed relieved, somehow, that that was all I wanted. He nodded his head and waved his hand with a gesture that meant, "Yes, all right, go ahead."

He was mumbling about the photographer's phone number, which he couldn't seem to find as I propelled myself up and out of the chair. I started for the door. Behind me, I heard him call out to his secretary. "Miss Teeler, where the hell is. . ." He stopped suddenly as if noticing my hand on the brick doorknob. "Kira!"

I turned to look back at him. "Yes, sir?"

"You go ask Frances, and you tell her that she can have the rest of the day off if she will come to your wedding."

I gave Mr. Dee a big smile and thanked him once again, but he was already yelling for Miss Teller to find his address book.

I found Frances taking a break in the coffee room. She had just had her nails done that morning. They were Indigo Illusion, she told me, as she held up her hands for me to see. There were little holograph peacock feathers at the ends. It was hard to pull her attention away from the beauty of her new nails, but when I started explaining about the wedding and about Cegan, Frances started listening.

Then she exploded. "Are you crazy? Girl, you must be desperate. There's hundreds of men I could have set you up with. All you had to do was ask me! I always figured, as serious as you are, that you were one of those career women determined to do without men. And all the time you were talking love sonnets to an alien you've never met? God, girl! Get out of fantasyland!"

Frances was gesturing with her hands. Her peacock nails were flying through the air. It was like one of the new kaleidoscope movies, where bits and pieces of information are supposed to make up a whole. I could see the birds on her fingers spreading out their multicolored wings and soaring into the sky. I tore my eyes away from the painted nails.

"I love him, Frances," I said. "I know it sounds unbelievable, but he's special — sweet, caring, and intelligent."

Frances shook her head, clucked like an old hen, and then put her arms around me. "You're a strange girl, Kira, and I think you're absolutely insane. But, sure, I'll be there for you. Hell, girl, I've married men worse than aliens! Who am I to talk?"

She forced me to eat some lunch when she discovered that I hadn't eaten since 4:00 A.M. I kept trying to tell her that I wasn't hungry, but I did feel better when I finished the egg on rye she ordered for me. With a diet cola in hand and a package of chips I hadn't even opened, I was ready to tell Cegan all the things I'd done that morning.

I think I half-expected that he'd say it had all been a ruse and that he really didn't want to marry me after all. I sat in my chair, alone in my room, and I didn't have the confidence to turn the switch on to let Cegan know I was there.

What if he didn't like what I'd done? What if he refused to go through with the wedding? What would I tell Mr. Dee, that nice attorney, and Frances? I sipped my cola and tried not to fret.

Somehow, Cegan knew I'd returned. He spoke to me in spite of the circuit indicating no connection. "Kira, you're back. Has Mr. Dee forbidden you to call me?"

"No. He said I could, but Cegan, do you still want to marry me?" I blurted out.

"Is this a Terran joke, Kira? If it is, I have failed to capture the humor."

"It's not a joke, Cegan. Do you still want to marry me?"

"With every breath, my siren. Why do you taunt me?"

"Then let's do it! I want to marry you. Mr. Dee has started working on the red tape if that's OK? Are you absolutely sure about it?"

"Kira, never ask that again. I will love you always. Do you pledge yourself as my wife, according to the Natharan Bridal Code, never having seen my face or my body, Kira?"

"Yes, Cegan. I love you, and I will marry you, no matter what."

"Thank you, my Kira," he said, and the sudden tension was gone.

I exhaled in relief, only just realizing that I'd been holding my breath from nervousness.

"You have honored me today, Kira, with your trust. I will never betray your love or the sacrifice of your heart. For all eternity, I will hold you in my soul, and I will cherish all that is you."

"Thank you, Cegan. I love you, too, forever and ever. And I will try to be a good wife, but I haven't had any practice, you know. And I really don't have the foggiest idea about what a Natharan wife is like . . .

"Cegan, would it be OK if the minister marries us at 4:30 today? Mr. Dee is setting it up, but we can change it if you don't want that time or something. Or if you want to wait . . ."

"From the moment of your pledge to me, Kira, you became my legal wife. That is according to the Natharan Bridal Code and the Law of the Marital Bond. Your word and mine were all that was needed to create the link that united our souls."

"Just the words that you said?"

"What more is needed than the exchange of our words to each other, my wife? However, I will acknowledge our marriage in whatever manner your Terran laws require and with whatever ceremony you deem necessary to establish our vows according to your beliefs. For that purpose, whatever pleases you, my wife, will please me as well."

And so it was; an hour and a half later, I was back in Mr. Dee's office when Frances pounced in, frowning at my dress. "Couldn't you have changed, at least?" she asked.

I shrugged. "I'm wearing a dress today, at least. That's better than blue jeans, isn't it? Besides, Cegan isn't here, remember, Frances. So it doesn't really matter what I wear."

It mattered to Frances. She ran off and returned minutes later with a huge, flowered scarf, which she insisted I must wear on my head as a veil. Then she handed me a blue rose she said she was lending me so I'd have something blue and something borrowed.

Mr. Dee, Miss Teeler, the secretary; Mr. Cronick, the attorney; a photographer named Simon; and Frances were all standing around in Mr. Dee's tiny office when the Rev. Samuel Livesey arrived. He was rather a handsome minister, tall and dark-haired, with a strong chin and a perfect nose. He was dressed nicely, too, in an expensive gray suit with a cleric's collar. I noticed Frances immediately eyeing his left ring finger. It was bare. Frances winked at me.

Rev. Livesey seemed confused at first as to who was getting married, but Mr. Dee explained again, and the Rev. only raised an eyebrow, shook his head, and then asked Cegan, via the transline, a few details that were important to know for the ceremony.

After Cegan assured the reverend that he'd never been married (prior to our private ceremony) and had no legal reason, according to New York State law, to be declared incapable of marriage, the Reverend wanted to know about Cegan's criminal record, his health, and the legal age of consent in Natharan. There was an edge to Cegan's voice, not irritation exactly, nor tension either, but perhaps impatience, as if he just wanted to be done with this so we could once more be alone in my office, talking.

Finally, the minister began the ceremony. He did not lecture us about religion, living together lovingly, or making the future brighter, as I'd heard at the weddings of my friends. He simply asked Cegan if he accepted me as his wife, and Cegan said, "Yes." Then the Rev. asked me if I accepted Cegan as my husband, and I said, "Yes."

Mr. Dee was told to kiss me in proxy. He planted the briefest touch of his lips on my forehead, and then the Rev. Livesey said, "Cegan, Captain of the Natharan vessel, the Streptha, and Kira Stevens, formerly from Roxanne, New York, as a representative of the State of New York, I hereby declare you officially husband and wife."

There was no final kiss, no breaking into organ music, and no formal conclusion to the service. I simply stepped forward, picked up the mike, and spoke into it softly so that, hopefully, only Cegan could hear.

"Thank you, Cegan, for taking part in this ceremony with me. I know for you it wasn't necessary, but it was important to me, and I appreciate that you were willing to marry me as a Terran. I'm going to say goodbye now, and I'll return to my room in a few minutes and talk with you then. I love you."

I hadn't flipped the switch for Cegan to speak. I hadn't known that he'd want to. "Kira, flip the switch, my siren," he said softly so only I could hear. "Of course, we needed to fulfill Terran requirements. How else could I hope to take you with me when I lead you to the stars?"

"But I thought . . ."

"Return quickly to me, My Love. We can talk easier when we are alone."

I clicked off the switch and disconnected my transystem from Mr. Dee's while the others watched. Mr. Cronick and Miss Teeler, a very tall, slender woman with a "killer dress," walked over and stood waiting for me to finish. Then, each of them kissed me lightly on the cheek and congratulated me.

Mr. Cronick asked once more for my signature, this time for the marriage certificate. I signed it and then turned to receive congratulations from Rev. Livesey and Frances. The Rev. pecked at my brow, but Frances threw her arms about me and hugged me so hard I thought I'd run out of air. Finally, Mr. Dee stepped up and taking my elbow in his hand, he pulled me gently over to the side of the room.

"It wasn't quite what you wanted, was it, Kira?" he said rather sadly.

"It was fine," I assured him. "Thank you for everything you've done. Cegan and I appreciate it."

Mr. Dee's hands stretched out to grip my arms, and he held me away from him, staring into my eyes. Finally, he shook his head slowly and said, "Kira, I hope this wasn't a mistake for you. If Cegan doesn't meet all those promises he made you, we'll get Mr. Cronick to draw up some divorce papers faster than the company moved on the wedding.

"You understand me? You won't have to stay with him, and we'll want you back in an executive position, little lady. With those pictures of Natharan and the story you're going to have after all this, you can name your price, and Transtel Systems will go for it. Now, don't you quote me on it. That's just between you and me. OK?"

"I don't want a divorce, Mr. Dee. I told you I love Cegan."

"I know, Kira. But it's good to have options, and I'll see that you have them. You go back to your office now, and you can talk all day long to that husband of yours. I'm going to relieve you from your duties from this point on."

"Please don't fire me, Mr. Dee. I want to keep working here, at least until Cegan comes."

"I have no intention of firing you! We want you on the payroll. I'm just telling you that you don't have to continue with your grid coordinate checks. Someone else can take over your lineups."

"But I want to do that. I like doing the checks and scheduling the appointments, and you said to yourself that I'm good at it. I mean, I know that someone had to cover for me yesterday and today, but . . ."

"All right," he said, throwing his hands up in the air. "But you let me know if it's too much for you, Kira. I just wanted you to have some time off before . . . What the hell, congratulations, my dear. Now, scoot."

"Thank you again, Mr. Dee. I think your daughter's awfully lucky to have you as her father," I said, and I threw my arms around his neck and kissed his cheek.

I walked back over to Frances then to give her back the borrowed blue rose and the scarf that had been my veil. I tried. Frances wouldn't take them.

"Keep them as souvenirs of your wedding," she told me. She was sitting on the Reverend's lap, one arm flung around his neck. Lipstick marks, like purple bruises, were multiplying on the poor man's cheek. I felt sorry for him. Simon, the photographer, was still taking pictures of everything.

I left and trudged slowly back to my office, thinking that I should feel different in some way. I was no longer single, either by Natharan standards or Terran. I had a husband. I was married. I kept whispering the words over and over, but they didn't sound real. They didn't sound like they were about me.

I returned to my office and sat down on the floor. Nightmagic was still laughing down at me. His rider still had perfect form. Why did I feel like nothing had changed?

Chapter Eight: Definition of Alien
Doesn't Belong to

For some reason, it was hard to talk to Cegan again. I didn't know what to say, and when I tried to speak, my words seemed stilted and artificial. I couldn't seem to make the transition from who I used to be to who I was now.

"Kira," Cegan said, breaking into my babble.

I stopped to listen. If Cegan had any wonders of wisdom to give me now, I was eager to hear. "Thank you," he said. It stopped my false-sounding gushes. I fell silent. "Kira," he continued. "When you accepted me as your husband, when you gave me your pledge, I felt your laughter inside me. It was like water bubbling up from the ground, rushing joyfully all about. It was the taste of fresh air and sunshine. It was the joy I felt at this moment.

"Jupiter is showing on my screen today, looking huge and red-streaked, with its giant rings of icy rock. When you said 'yes' in your Earth ceremony, my eyes looked up, and, for that moment, it felt like the largest planet of your system was witness to my joy. I know it is not so. The inanimate has no life or ability to perceive, but perhaps the overflow of the love in my heart brought about the illusion."

"You weren't angry? I thought you sounded vexed or impatient, at least, because Rev. Livesey was asking you all those questions."

"I can never be impatient with something that is important to you, Kira. However, it is possible that I was not skillful at hiding the annoyance in my heart. It was not easy having another in my place whose arms were free to hold you and whose lips touched yours when I could not."

"He didn't kiss me like that, Cegan. It was a fatherly kiss on the forehead. Are Natharans jealous?"

"Irrelevant. My wife is Terran, and the thought of her in the arms of another drives thorns into me."

"Thorns, Cegan?"

"Swords, long knives, heavy sticks . . . "

"Cegan, I wish you were here with me now."

"I, too, taste the sadness of our separation."

"Is that Natharan, 'to taste the sadness'? Is that the way a Natharan talks, or is it you, Cegan?"

"It is Natharan, I suppose, but it is you, my wife, who guides the words. There is no power in language without purpose."

"And what is the purpose, Cegan?"

"To share a thought, to trade our feelings. Is that not the purpose of language?"

"Yes, but when you say the words, they sound profound. When I say them, they feel unfinished and unsure."

"Feelings are always unsure until they are spoken. That is the reason why they need to be expressed, Kira. Oftentimes, it is the articulation of the words that move us forward. And, therefore, my wife, they are never finished because they are forever changing."

"Is that Natharan philosophy?"

"Yes. Would you prefer Natharan poetry instead?"

"I'd love to hear a Natharan poem!"

"This one is not elaborate. It is a children's poem:

A moment shared,

Is the rainbow heralded,

The sunset viewed,

The water savored."

Tears trickled down my cheeks. It wasn't the poem. It was just being overwhelmed with the day and with the sweetness of Cegan. His words were making me ache inside. I wanted to be with him so badly. I wanted to feel his arms around me.

"Kira, you are crying. Why?"

"Because I love you, and because your words are always so beautiful, and because I want to touch your hand so much it hurts," I cried.

"Ah, My Kira. Know this, my love has grown wider than the inky blackness I see between us. I close my eyes, and I can almost reach your hand. Do you not feel my touch?"

"Yes, Cegan," I said, closing my eyes and holding out my hand.

Within white office walls and a ship in space, two souls stretched out their hands, and I believe our fingers clasped. Maybe it was no more than longing or imagination, but, for the space of that moment, I felt Cegan with me.

We talked through the evening and long into the night. I told him about the visit of Thenus Sachem. "It meant so much to my father and me to speak with him. Just to have someone who knows you. It made you more real. Thank you for sending him.

"I never told you this, Cegan, but my room in the apartment has holographic stars over my bed so I can gaze at the suns from many galaxies and pretend that I am looking out into space. I used to lie in my bed staring up at those fake stars and wonder if you were an illusion, just like them."

"I understand, Kira. I reach out so often to you in the dark, and you slip away each time. I wake in yearning and wonder which is the dream and which the truth."

"Fly faster, Cegan. Come sooner, please."

"If I could, I would be there now," he said, and in his voice, I heard all the longing I had hoped to hear. I left my chair and went to sit on the floor. Thanks to Natharan technology, our voices carried from anywhere in the world, and Cegan often told me he liked thinking about me, not at a desk, but on the floor, grasping my knees to my chest.

"Tell me more of Thenus' visit, and what your father said," he requested.

I wanted to tell Cegan about the visit, but first, I had to explain my dad. It was important for Cegan to know how wonderful my Dad was, how he always offered money but glowed with pride when I refused it, how he had wanted me to stay on the farm but accepted when I wouldn't, and how he'd told me, "Go fly your wings, Child, but always remember where home is."

I tried to explain to Cegan about the unlit pipe and why it made me love my father more, knowing how Dad still honored the pledge he'd made to my mother. I cried when I reached the part about how sad I'd made my dad when I told him I was marrying an alien.

"I am sorry, Kira, that I have been the cause of your father's unhappiness, but every father must face the day when his daughter leaves him to be with her chosen one."

How could I explain to Cegan that there was more to it? How could I say that I feared my father would never accept Cegan, never trust him? I wanted my father to accept Cegan more than anything. I wanted him to see how wonderful Cegan was. But I couldn't tell Cegan of those fears and desires, so instead, I spoke of the visit.

"Cegan, Mr. Sachem tried to talk me out of marrying you."

"But he could not convince you to do so," Cegan said. "Why is there anger in your voice?"

"Because he was not a friend to you in the things he said."

"Kira, he went to you. That he did in friendship. I thanked him for it when I talked with him later." The sound of Cegan's smile entered into his words. "Thenus has become another of your protectors. Do you collect these 'knights in shining armor' with your siren's voice?"

I heard the smile, yet, for me, the words had a sting. "I didn't ask for his protection!" Cegan ignored my words temporarily. "Mr. Sachem attempted to persuade me as well. He told me that I should not allow your sacrifice, as he put it. 'In Kira's eyes,' he said, 'there is a trusting innocence.' Those were his exact words, Kira, and the way he said them, I knew it was a compliment to you. With eyes like that, Kira, it is no wonder that males fall down at your feet, begging to serve you."

I stood up to pace. I was suddenly restless and irritated. "Stop it, Cegan. I know you are teasing me, but I don't like it."

"Ah, Kira," Cegan cooed. "Was I teasing? Does a husband on your planet not delight in the praise of his wife?"

If Cegan had been in the room, he would have seen my eyes flash and my head arch in the challenge. "I am not straight off the farm, as they say in the city. I have lived on my own for seven months. I do not need the protection of men. And I wouldn't know what husbands . . ." I broke it off there. I actually knew very well what husbands took delight in, but we hadn't been talking about that.

"Kira," Cegan soothed. "Easy, my sweet siren. Thenus only spoke the truth as he saw it. There was no intention of harm in his friendship."

I remained quiet. I couldn't agree, but I wouldn't argue with Cegan over Mr. Sachem.

Cegan was silent for a moment before he began to speak. "I have been reading a book on the history of the women's fight for equality. I find it very interesting."

There was a point Cegan was making. I knew him well enough to know that. Yet, how we'd gone from Mr. Sachem to women's lib was confusing. "Are you for or against?" I asked. It was an important issue. I couldn't believe I was just now asking.

"Kira." How could someone put so much meaning in one word? Usually, when Cegan said my name, it was musical or like a poem he savored. Just then, he'd said it like, "Stop it."

"The book is helping me to analyze the psychology of your culture," he informed me.

"I can understand that Cegan, but you have to have an opinion on it. You do believe that women are equal to men, don't you?"

"No."

"Oh, my God!" I cried out. I'd been married for two hours, and I already needed a divorce. Why hadn't I asked Cegan this before? How could I have been so stupid?

"Kira." Again, he gave me the "stop it" version of my name. I halted my pacing to hear what Cegan had to say in his defense.

"Kira, equal means 'the same, evenly balanced proportionally with a correspondence in all respects.' I am sure you understand that by your Terran definition I cannot agree with you. Women and men are not equal. They are very different."

I could breathe again. I had misunderstood. Cegan was, at times, so literal that I often had to remember to sort through my words for more precise meanings.

He continued, "The nature of each gender differs considerably. This book does not analyze that dissimilarity adequately."

"Cegan, what are you saying?" I was puzzled but no longer as fearful of what I'd hear. My fingers twirled the blue rose that Frances had given me. It released a spray of rose perfume. I breathed in the fragrance with delight.

"I am saying, Siren, that Mr. Dee and Mr. Sachem honor you in feeling the need to protect you. Contrary to what this book states, their feelings are not an insult. It is the opposite, Kira. Their desire to protect you reflects their high respect for you."

"It's respect when they think I cannot take care of myself?"

"Kira, would you prefer that they were indifferent?"

I sighed. "Just not interfering." I taped the artificial rose on the wall next to the picture of Dad. It was nice to have a keepsake, even if it had not been the wedding of my dreams. I placed the wedding certificate beside it.

The smile was back in Cegan's words. "I am grateful to both of them. Their interference has brought about the attainment of our marriage."

I couldn't disagree with that. I just wasn't fond of their lectures.

After a moment, Cegan continued. "Thenus fears that you will not adapt to life on Natharan."

I had been draping my new flowered scarf around my shoulders. I took it off and started to protest. I didn't know if I could adapt, but I resented it when people thought they could make predictions about me, especially when they didn't even know me well.

Cegan didn't wait for my protest. He continued. "I reassured Thenus that whether you adapted well or not to Natharan was not important because if you do not like my home, Kira, we will spend little time there. I told that to Thenus, but he was still concerned.

He said he did not believe that you would adapt to a spacer's life because you were used to being close to nature. Again, I assured him, Kira, that if you were unable to find happiness on the ship, we would find another path.

"You have married me, Kira, but that marriage is not a trap. If you are unhappy, we can try something else. If it is I you cannot accept, then I will free you. I would not be content, Kira, to see you wilt in misery. Do you understand, my wife?"

I breathed out a sigh. I hadn't realized that I was still frightened by it all. Cegan had once again known just what to say. "I will be happy, no matter where we are, if we are together," I told him.

"If you can accept me?" Cegan persisted.

"I have accepted you," I said, indignant, even though I knew the big test had yet to come.

"You have not lain beside me and touched my body," Cegan warned me.

"Nor have you. What if you find me ugly?"

"Then I am looking at you with the wrong eyes."

I sighed. How beautifully he always said things. "Cegan, I want to be with you and feel your arms about me, but what if I see you with the wrong eyes?"

"Then I will be patient."

"You will wait for my fear to leave?" I asked, dreadfully afraid that I would fail him.

"I will wait for you as long as it takes, my wife, as long as you need."

It was hard to go home that evening. A bride should not spend her wedding night alone. I lay down in my single bed, and I stared at the stars above my bed. I pretended that they were real and that Cegan was up there in the dark of the ceiling between the spheres of light, and he was looking down at me. I closed my eyes then and slept.

Chapter Nine: Definition of Alien, *Not Connected*

I continued working, talking late into the evenings with Cegan and arriving early so we could greet the day together, and all was wonderful between us. I was more positive than ever that I'd done the right thing in marrying him. I loved the way Cegan expressed himself, and I clung to his words long after the transline was off when I was driving home or lying in my bed at night.

I was becoming very impatient for the day of Cegan's arrival. I told him what I planned to wear so he would know me the moment he saw me. I told him how I'd wear my hair and where I was planning on standing. I explained how my father would be with me, probably glued to my side, and how Dad would probably be wearing his blue jeans and looking just like a farmer straight off his tractor, but a very handsome one.

Then, I blabbed on, explaining all the things I wanted to show Cegan. I suggested that we should go to the zoo first so he could see all the Terran animals, and then I told him I'd take him to the Statue of Liberty. And, of course, we'd go to the United Nations building because we Terrans were all so proud of the work being done there. I listed all the museums that Cegan would enjoy and told him about the nightclubs and the live Broadway shows.

I never noticed that Cegan was very noncommittal about all my ideas. I just assumed he'd want to go. I think the idea of my being his tour guide did please him. But he never mentioned, and it never occurred to me, that it might be dangerous for us to do those things together. And no one had told me that it might not be safe for outworlders to roam about freely.

I guess Cegan thought he was protecting me by not warning me what to expect, or perhaps he just didn't want to hurt my feelings because I was so enthusiastic. For whatever reason, he let me ramble and said little that day, but I do remember his telling me that Earth looked like a friendly giant's head peering into his ship's screen.

I laughed so hard when I heard him say that. It was that picture of a big, grinning giant peering in at him that I held in my mind throughout the turmoil that rocked the next day.

All that night, I couldn't sleep. It was the last day before Cegan's arrival, and I was thrilled, anxious, and excited. I was up and dressed by 3:00 A.M. and at Transtel Systems by 5:00 A.M. (Cegan never seemed to mind if I disturbed him. In fact, he told me once that he liked to lie in bed talking to me. I remember how the idea of an alien in a bed had made me smile the first time, but I couldn't think where else he could "catch his forty winks.")

Anyway, that day was when Frances "cracked". After spending her usual intimate night with a red-hot flame, she let slip the story about what she'd witnessed in Mr. Dee's office. Her date that evening happened to be a reporter for the New York Star, and, on hearing about the proxy ceremony, he threw himself out of their bed and raced to the newspaper office. And so, like a hurricane buffeting all the trees and houses in its path, the media descended on our marriage.

All the morning papers carried news of the Alien-Terran wedding that had taken place at Transtel Systems. And, suddenly, although I didn't know it until much later, my life became a public exhibition.

At 7:23 in the morning, newsmen with cameras invaded Transtel Systems. Guards on the first floor stopped them from going further. An extremely perturbed Mr. Dee escorted them out and then called the police to ask for assistance.

An announcement was issued over the intercom of Transtel Systems that no one would be permitted to leave the building until further notice. I was just trying to figure out what was wrong when Mr. Dee came into my office and sat down with me. It was he who told me about Frances and the deluge of newsmen.

Cegan was on the line, and he began asking detailed questions about the company's ability to protect me.

"I don't need protection," I assured them both. "I simply won't talk to the reporters."

Mr. Dee started stuttering: "You, you . . ."

He turned red. But he didn't have a chance to speak because Cegan was already admonishing me. I quickly flipped the switch so Mr. Dee wouldn't see that Cegan had spoken before he should have.

"It brings me great joy that your nature is trusting, my wife, but there are Terrans who will not share your tolerances. Some of them will be dangerous, and you must do exactly as Mr. Dee says."

"Dangerous, why? I don't understand."

Mr. Dee stopped stuttering. He moaned loudly and shook his head. "Ay, the young are so foolish!" He was tugging at his neck, pulling on the yellow-and-brown-striped tie that picked up the colors in his jacket so well.

"I will expect a police escort for my wife from this point on," Cegan demanded. "She is to go no place without a full guard."

"What?" I yelped.

"He's right, Kira. Tell Cegan I'm going right now to make the calls," Mr. Dee yelled back over his shoulder as he went storming out of the room. "And, Kira," he said, popping back in, "you are not to go anywhere. Do not leave this room, understand?"

My mouth dropped open. I didn't have time to argue. He was gone too quickly. I turned away from the door and started to complain to Cegan.

"You don't need to use the uh . . . john . . . uh . . . restroom, do you, Kira?" Mr. Dee asked, poking his head back through the doorway.

"No."

"I'll take you if you need to . . . better use it now if . . ."

"No, thank you, Mr. Dee. I'm fine."

"OK, just thought I'd check. Remember. You're not to leave this room, OK?"

"I don't see the need . . ." It was pointless. Mr. Dee had once more vanished.

"What is all this about, Cegan? I don't understand. I don't need policemen following me around! No one's threatening me. And it's nobody's business who I marry!"

"Have you called your father, Kira?" Cegan asked instead of answering my rampage.

"Oh, no! My poor dad! Thank you, Cegan. I've got to get off. OK?"

"I love you, Kira," Cegan said, and the light blinked out.

I dialed my father's number. I knew it was time to tell him the truth about the wedding. I needed to let him know before he heard it from someone else. The phone rang and rang. I was beginning to think he wasn't there when he finally answered.

"Kira, are you OK?" he wanted to know.

"Yes, but I have to tell you . . ."

"That you married the alien? Reporters already told me." My father's voice was as deflated as his body had been the day I'd first told him about Cegan. It made me feel very guilty. My cowardice had caused Dad so much pain!

"Oh, Dad, I'm sorry. I should have told you. Please forgive me."

"Of course, Kira. It's done and over. What time is the alien arriving?"

"His name is Cegan, Dad, and he's supposed to land around 6:00 tomorrow morning."

"I see. Are you at Transtel Systems now? I want you to promise me that you will stay in that building. Don't go outside for any reason. I'm leaving right this moment, and I'll come get you. Promise me, Kira?"

"I promise, Dad. I won't go anywhere."

He disconnected, and I sat there holding the phone for several minutes before I could release it. When I pried my fingers off and placed it down on the desk, I wanted to cry. An awful ache was welling up behind my eyes, but no tears came. Why hadn't I prepared my father? How could I have let a stranger tell him what I should have had the courage to say?

"Kira," Cegan said, no longer pretending that the Terran system had control of his use of it. "Kira, my love, I understand your sadness. Your pain is rippled across my heart."

"I should have told him, Cegan. I should have told him," I kept repeating, but I could no longer hold back the tears. They were pouring freely.

"Feel my arms around you, my wife. Lean your head against my chest. I shall take your pain if you will allow me."

I leaned against the wall instead. The coolness of it helped absorb my tears. I breathed in deeply. "I was so stupid, Cegan."

"Never, my Siren. The sharks of your media are often bloodthirsty. It was inevitable that they would attack your father. I am sorry that I was the cause of it."

"Oh, Cegan. It's not your fault. You told me to tell him!"

"Kira, as your father said, 'it's done and over.'"

"You heard?"

"Will you forgive me for listening?"

"Of course, but I don't understand how you can . . ."

"I am thankful that you arrived at your office early this morning, Kira. Had you been late or stayed at home today, I convulse to think of the damage the media would have done to your trust. It was my error. I should have considered one of the witnesses breaking the pledge to silence. I ask for your forgiveness."

"Why? None of this is your fault."

"No, that is not correct. The responsibility was mine, my wife. You are untutored in alien relations and innocent of the harsh possibilities of this situation. It was my experience that you relied on, and I failed you."

"Cegan, how could you predict what my world would do? I should have thought about Frances telling someone."

"Ah, my wife. Without xxxxxxx, it is true that the light of honesty is within you. You honor me daily with your grace."

"Cegan, I . . ."

"Permit me, Kira, to justify that I believed that this problem would not begin until I landed. That is not a valid excuse for my failure to begin your training. I should have prepared you for a variety of probable repercussions."

"What training?"

Cegan didn't answer. Instead, he apologized abruptly for needing to disconnect and said that he would return shortly. He sounded concerned about leaving me alone, but I was honestly glad. I needed time to think about all that was happening.

I'd argued with Cegan about my protectors, as he called them. I'd thought that I could take care of myself and didn't need their help, but I was finding out that wasn't true. With all that was happening, I was frightened and confused.

Perhaps Mr. Dee and Mr. Sachem were right about my inexperience. Maybe I was not as citified as I'd thought. I guess it was stupid of me to believe that my marriage with Cegan was only a private matter. I'd thought that all I had to do was to make the decision on whether to marry him or not. Why had I never thought about others playing a part in it?

And the number of people involved kept growing. Mr. Dee said that now even the government wanted to talk with me about Cegan. I didn't want to talk to them. Could they make me? Would they put me in jail if I refused?

Mr. Dee interrupted my pacing by bringing in a small TV, the kind that only held one panel at a time. "Here," he said. "If you want to see what's brewing outside, you can watch it, but if it bothers you, Kira, just keep it off and wait for it to settle down."

"Mr. Dee, when are the people from the government arriving? Do I really have to talk with them?"

Mr. Dee smiled. "No, your Captain Cegan has already taken care of that. He called through to me, and I patched him to the necessary departments. He is very protective of you, Kira. The way he demanded around the clock guards for your protection and then wouldn't allow those officials to bother you, and he even thought to order a police escort for your father, whom he tells me is on his way.

"There is a possibility that I was wrong about him, Kira, although I still believe that marrying outside of your species is foolish. Still, I have no criticism of the way he has handled this situation. He is more knowledgeable of Terran behaviors and customs and more perceptive to your needs than any alien has the right to be."

"Cegan ordered my dad protected, too?" I sighed. I really didn't have a clear picture of what was going on. Had everyone gone crazy?

"That's just the beginning of it. Your captain had a whole list of demands about your protection at Space Port tomorrow, and every time one of those government officials said it couldn't be done that way, your captain explained clearly how that was how it was going to be handled.

That captain of yours never once took 'no' as an answer. I think he finally just wore down all their excuses. The government bureaucrats ended up agreeing to every single one of the captain's demands."

"Thank you, Mr. Dee, for telling me all that. I don't think Cegan would have mentioned it. He seems to think that the less I know, the better it is, but that's not true."

Mr. Dee raised his hands into the air and laughed. "I don't want to be involved in any squabbles between you two. At least, not the kind that are the normal domestic ones."

Mr. Dee's expression was so funny. He was standing there looking like he was a victim of a hold-up. His bushy gray eyebrows were peaked like the Matterhorn, and his eyes were bulging. A second later, his smile was jolly again, and I knew he'd only been trying to tease me into laughter.

"Mr. Dee, have I told you how wonderful I think you are?"

"You're a sweet girl, Kira. Come, I'll take you to the restroom now. And no argument, or I'll complain to your father. Deal?"

The guards, there were four of them for heaven's sake, also escorted me to the Ladies' Room. It was all so embarrassing, but I suppose I was lucky they didn't insist on following me inside. When I exited, we marched back to my office like a parade with no music.

I was too uncomfortable to turn around and look at the two men behind me, but I knew from my first glance that all four had the same shiny black suits, pale blue shirts, and ties of varying striped patterns of blue. They were all of about the same height and even their haircuts looked similar, except the one on the front right had long sideburns.

I started to go into my office, but I couldn't help asking, "How come the police couldn't send at least one woman?"

The men shot glances at each other, and I could tell that they were uncomfortable with the question. Finally, one of them spoke up. "I think they were all busy."

"Why don't you tell her the truth," the one with the long sideburns said. "You might as well know, Ms. Stevens, every woman on the bureau refused."

The man in the back, whose eyes had not stopped patrolling the hall, snapped, "Our purpose here is not to entertain Ms. Stevens but to protect her. I suggest that we commence doing that, men."

Mr. Dee reached over and patted my head. "Don't worry about it, Kira. I'm going to go get you a nice, fattening cinnamon roll. That will take your mind off all this," he said as he left.

I thought about the women all refusing. What did that mean? Why should they care if I was married to an alien? It was strange, as strange as everything else happening that day.

I ordered the little TV to find NYCB, New York City Broadcasting Co., the station where there was always news. Mr. Dee had told me that there were people assembling outside the New York Transtel Systems building, but I didn't expect anything like what I saw on the translinecast.

A massive crowd was gathered, with people milling about, talking, and shouting, all looking angry and passionately involved. A newsman was telling the watchers that there were over three hundred people present, and more were arriving at each moment. He acted excited by the prospect and seemed to be encouraging the viewers to come join in the "party."

"Here you are," Mr. Dee said, carrying in my sweet roll and a big cup of coffee. He handed them to me and looked over at the screen. Broadcasters were busy telling the viewers the facts about my life. Videos of me riding Powder, my horse, around barrels, pictures of my dance team, and even interviews with some of my high school teachers were being translinevised.

"Now, that's courageous," Mr. Dee said when he saw me handling a rearing Powder after some brainless kid had thrown a paper airplane across the arena. "I wouldn't get on an animal like that for a million dollars!"

"Powder's sweet, Mr. Dee. He just got scared. All horses do that when a paper goes flying by."

"I can't bear to watch," Mr. Dee said, and once more, he patted my head and left.

News cameras began to interject shots of individuals in the crowd out in front of Transtel Systems. For some reason, opinions about the Alien-Terran marriage were being collected. I heard myself being called "desperate," "stupid," "traitor," "alien lover," and "sick groupie."

Some of the crowd in the background were screaming curse words at Cegan and yelling for him to go home. Others were yelling out things about me. One of the interviewees held up his Bible and said he was praying for me. Another stepped forward and told the cameraman that he'd marry me to save me from my sins.

I ordered a panel change and asked for another news station. The next one showed the Space Port, where a Baskante had just been attacked by a maddened citizen. The man who'd attacked had struck the alien with a butter knife. It had done no damage to the Baskante's slightly metallic skin, but the Space Port had called in the military, and full guards were to be assigned to all extraterrestrials.

What had I done? Had I endangered all extraterrestrials just because of my marriage to Cegan? Had I set back the progress of interworld trading? What if more aliens were hurt? Would it be my fault?

"Anger is stirring everywhere," the newscaster said, airing shots taken from Space Ports across the globe. In Japan, there were riots at their Space Port, and picketers were asking the authorities to shut down the inflow of ships. They were demanding that all aliens be deported immediately.

In London, the Space Port was crowded with protesters pushing and shoving at the cordons of police. The camera lens focused on a Canonen, a member of a tall, slender race with bug eyes and droopy ears, who was just exiting his ship. Hundreds of spectators jeered and booed at him. "Go home, Go home!" they said. "Leave our women alone."

The panel returned to a local image. A tall, burly man with shaggy, gray paintbrush-looking eyebrows was being dragged off by the police. In the picture, you could see him struggling against their hold, and his face was all clenched up in anger, his mouth moving in a tirade of curses, which the broadcasters had thankfully cut off. "Serge Falisko, the alleged stabber of an alien, is seen here being hauled off to jail . . ."

The cameras moved to the Baskante. He was sitting on a chair in the Alien's Center with newsmen all about him. There were police, too, in their black uniforms and government men. You could tell the latter by their suspicious, shifting eyes as they surveyed the room, paying no attention to the little alien in front of them.

The Baskante's silver skin was no longer shiny, and his ears were tilted with stress. His eyes, twice the size of normal, were weepy with his anguish.

"Fine, am I," he told the camera. "No wish, I wife of Earth. Have already I in Baska wife."

I flipped the switch on my light, wanting to see if Cegan was available to talk with me. I wanted to tell him that he must not land. It wasn't safe for him. But, although I flipped it twice, Cegan didn't come on.

I ordered another panel change and listened for a moment to a medical show. The program had a psychiatrist discussing the neurotic tendencies of young females who were deprived of their mothers at an early age. It took me several minutes before I realized that I was the key player in their discussion.

I was just about to change the station when a second doctor, a psychotherapist, who was also sitting around the horseshoe table, began to speak. I paused a moment to listen to his opinion. He mentioned me at the very beginning of his dialogue and said that I was suffering from "maladjustment syndrome" because I had, in essence, been uprooted from a rural atmosphere and was attempting to adapt to an urban atmosphere, and, in my inability to adjust, I was going through a kind of culture shock.

"Otherwise," he said, "this Kira Stevens would not have been in the least interested in wedding some freak of nature from another planet."

"Freak of nature! How dare you say that, you creep!" I yelled.

One of the guards poked his head through the door. "You all right?" he asked.

He was the one with long sideburns. "No, I'm not all right," I told him. "The world has gone nuts!"

He gave me a grin and withdrew.

I ordered the doctors, who were still blabbing their pseudo-science garbage, to silence and flipped through the other stations. There were three daytime dramas revealing the lives of characters who had nonstop problems. An exercise program was on another station; a children's educational enlightenment hour and an instructional program on "Components of Sound and Light Physics" completed my choices.

I went back to the crowd scene outside the Transtel System building. The interviews were still in progress. A woman with bright red hair that spiked out into molded forms of animals was saying that she believed that I would never go through with it. "Once that alien steps off the ship, that Kira Stevens will start to screamin', and I bet she doesn't stop 'til she gets home where she belongs."

"That's not true," I told her, but, of course, she couldn't hear me. The crowd was whooping and cheering, and the woman, glowingly proud that she'd had her moment in the spotlight, blended back into the crowd.

A man of about my age stepped forward to the mike. He had dye-painted his skin purple, and it clashed brazenly with the red jumpsuit he had on. "Kira and I used to date," he said.

"What! I've never even seen you before!" I yelled at him.

"Yes, she's quite a swinger. One time, we were nude up on top of the UN building, where we'd sneaked in, and we were getting it on, and . . ."

"Oh, God, don't let my father hear him!" I said. I got on the phone right away to talk to Mr. Dee about suing the liar. He said he'd talk to the lawyer about it, and he calmed me down. (The company did, in the end, disprove that the purple guy had ever even met me, but that was days later, and in the meantime, my name kept getting smeared worse and worse until even my father probably didn't know what to believe.)

The camera moved on to the next interviewees. It took us in close to a pair of girls of perhaps fifteen or sixteen, both with straight blonde hair tinged in lime green and tied to the side. Each girl had a tattooed high school insignia on her face. The slightly taller one had her cougar done in purple, the other in orange. The girls were wearing cute little jumpsuits of polka-dotted yellows, oranges, and purples.

They were gushing in sentences with plenty of "Oh, my cosmos" and "This is so colossal!" They were saying how romantic they thought that my falling in love with an alien was. The crowd, hearing their comments, suddenly went wild. People started heckling the girls, and then, like the giant swell of an ocean wave, a surge of bodies pushed the teenagers down and swallowed them up. There was screaming and panic, and the camera swung all about, but the girls were no longer visible. There was only the restless mob and a sea of irate faces.

Then, the camera swung to follow an ambulance, blazing its way towards the scene. Helmeted policemen with electric padded buffers on their chests strode into the mass in search of the girls. The crowd went berserk, yet still respectful of the shock a body in contact with the policeman's buffer would bring. A path miraculously appeared down the middle of the crowd, and the policemen and the ambulance personnel they escorted made their way to the place where the girls had last been seen.

A cameraman must have braved the path as well because the limp bodies of the two girls were filmed lying on the gray and blooded cement. Stretchers extended, and the bodies were lifted onto them and then wheeled back to the flashing ambulance.

I was just ordering the TV off when the "official protestors" arrived. These were from the "Keep Earth for Earth people" faction. They somehow cleared a place in the sidewalk in front of Transtel Systems, which only a moment before had been filled with the curious and angry. They began marching back and forth, carrying their wooden post signs. One board accused me of being a traitor to my planet. Another poster even had my name on it: 'Kira Stevens, go home!' it said. A third said, "What's wrong with Earthmen?"

"Off," I said, angry enough to kick the TV.

"You are OK, Kira?" Cegan asked, making me jump with the suddenness of his voice.

"No. I don't think I can do this, Cegan! I don't want my name being carried back and forth with all those terrible things they're saying. And there are people lying about me and people getting hurt. And all the outerworlders are being insulted.

"Please don't land here, Cegan. A Baskante got hurt. I couldn't bear for someone to stab you. Maybe we should meet somewhere else. You could fly to another country, or maybe my government could fly me up to you, or maybe . . ."

"Kira, shh! Do you trust me?"

"Oh, Cegan, I trust you. It's everybody else. They've gone crazy. I don't know why. None of this makes sense."

"Trust me, Kira. Do as I tell you. Close your eyes. Are they closed?"

"Yes."

"Good. Keep them shut and listen to my voice. Forget about everything else. Breathe deeply, Kira. In and out, slowly. Are you doing that?"

"Yes."

"I need you to relax, my Siren, to calm down and forget the madness. There are only you and I here in this room and the love we feel for each other. You and I are bonded, Kira; always remember that.

And that bond is stronger than knives and sharp words or lies. We are together, my wife.

"What anyone else says can have no power against our union, nor against the way we feel. Shut out those hate-mongers. Don't listen to their words, Kira. Their words are only the sound and the substance of Terran fear. Remember our talks? These people have permitted their phobias to dominate their Conscious Minds. Forgive them, Kira, but do not heed them.

"You, my wife, are beyond that. You have the light of honesty, remember? Do not allow their terror to feed your anxiety. Remember that our love is stronger than all the hate and fear that flows about your planet.

"Soon, if you will let me, I will put my arms around you, and we will know the comfort of two hearts beating as one. Will you have that courage, Kira? Will you remember that it is I who loves you and that this body I wear is only the shell for my soul?

"Do not fear for my safety, my love. I will not be in danger. It is you who must take special care. I have talked with your government. They will guard you. This, they have promised me. But you must follow their orders. You must do exactly as they say. Will you do this for me, my wife?"

"Yes. And thank you, Cegan, for talking with them. I didn't want to be questioned by the Bureau. When Mr. Dee told me that you took care of it and you spoke to them for me, I was so relieved. Thank you!"

"I wish I could take more of your burden away, Kira. If it were in my power, I would not tolerate this abuse of you, but I am too far away to shelter you from it. "

"Cegan, I don't need to be sheltered."

"I am not stepping on the toes of your womanhood, Kira. You are simply far too young to have officials and newsmen overwhelming you with their demands.

I should have been irritated, but I had to smile over the translation. Sometimes, I even forgot that Cegan spoke another language.

"I am relieved that your father will be at your side for most of the turmoil. Lean on him for strength, Kira. Even the trunk of the strongest tree can be battered and toppled by a storm."

"He won't give me any choice about that," I assured Cegan.

"Yes, I think I shall enjoy knowing your father when he is no longer angry with me."

"That's going to take a long time, Cegan."

"It will come, Kira. We will be patient, won't we?"

Cegan didn't wait for me to respond. He probably knew I would have argued. He continued, "And when I land tomorrow, no matter what happens, Kira, I will guarantee your safety. It is more difficult when you are not by my side, but I will assure you, even if you fear me too much to enter my ship, you will never be allowed to come to physical harm because of your vows. This, I promise you.

"But even Natharan technology cannot protect you from evil words and malicious lies. So, tomorrow, you must listen only to your Rational Mind, Kira, as I have instructed you. And you must know me as I have taught you to know me. I am Cegan, the Natharan, the one who gave you his bond forever."

"I'm not real good with the Rational Mind stuff, Cegan . . ."

He sighed, an almost human sigh of exasperation. "Kira, my wife, I know that, and we will work on it. However, tomorrow, if your fear

159

of me when you see me makes you want to run from me, close your eyes and remember our talks. You must hold onto the trust you have gathered from the words that passed between us.

"Think on the day you gave your pledge, your vow to accept me, no matter how our bodies differed. Remember that I am the one who loves you and that I will never hurt you. Believe, instead, that I will protect you and help you through all this, that I will provide for all your needs.

"Above all, you must trust me, Kira, even though the world seems mad. Many who are full of fear and hate will be overpowered by their phobias and will spout lies and half-truths that will make you doubt yourself and me. You must withstand their tyranny and walk to me, Kira, placing your hand in mine, concentrating on what you feel for me, knowing that my love burns for you beneath whatever outer form you see. Can you do that, Kira?"

"I love you, Cegan. That I know. I will try to trust, and I will try not to listen to the picketers. I don't know that I can promise more than that. I'm Terran, and I still suffer from all those phobias you've told me about."

"Ah, but Kira, you are now Natharan as well. And Natharans look into the soul."

"Are Natharans ever scared?"

"Of course, Kira."

I am sure he could have used my question as a chance to expound on Natharan's philosophy, but he didn't. Instead, Cegan talked about a penetat, which, as far as I could discern, is a cross between a koala bear and a monkey. He told me how this house pet likes to climb up on light fixtures and must be trained not to plummet down on guests who drop in.

I laughed when he narrated the story about a visiting representative from Qweldon who jumped straight upwards at least six feet in his surprise at the pet's mischievousness and thus accidentally trained the family's penetat never again to drop down on guests.

"Does your family have one?" I askcd.

"I am sad to say that we have no pets at all."

That day, for some reason, I laughed more than usual, and we talked about the silliest things. I told Cegan all the jokes I knew, and he told me some of his. The following is an example of Natharan humor. If any of them were funny, I sure didn't get the punch lines:

"Two males were marching across rocky terrain. The first slipped and fell. The second fell over the first, so they lay there on the rocky soil and argued about who was more to blame. When the sky darkened, and three of the moons cast enough light for them to walk again, the first one said, 'I will help you up because the blame was mostly mine.'

" 'No,' said the second, 'I will help you up because the blame was mostly mine.'

"When the sky lightened, and the two suns rose, the first one said, 'I will assist you in standing because the blame is mostly mine.'

"The second one said, 'No, I will assist you in standing because the blame is mostly mine.' And from that day to this, the two are still arguing as they lay there in the rocky soil."

No wonder Natharans don't know how to laugh!

As I said, I told Cegan my favorite jokes and his reception was about the same. I guess we will have to learn from each other about humor in different worlds.

As we batted topics about, debating, and arguing in a joking manner, I kept wishing I had the courage to tell Cegan how much I longed for his lips on mine, but I did not know if it was true. And, in between the bits and pieces of trivia, Cegan kept assuring me of his love, yet I heard the tension in his voice. And, although I knew he'd never admit it, I could tell he was just as nervous as I was about our meeting when he landed.

When my father finally arrived, he had the escort Cegan had ordered for him. How they found my father on his drive into the big city is a wonder to both Dad and me. Still, police escort or not, Dad had to fight his way through the crowds and city police just to enter the parking garage. His name was on the list for entrance. Mr. Dee had made sure of that, but there was apparently still a lot of checking and double-checking. And even though Dad showed the proper I.D., they still scanned his retina and took a blood sample to check his DNA. Poor Dad!

Then, when Dad made his way into the building, escorted by four members of the police, Mr. Dee met my father and grilled him again about his identity. Finally, at last, convinced that my dad was the real Mr. Stevens, Mr. Dee, and Dad supposedly fell into a rather odd conversation about headstrong daughters. They were just finishing that conversation as they walked through my door.

However, just before that, Cegan and I had been discussing why Natharans couldn't swim in the Natharan oceans when suddenly, two guards charged into the office, waving their guns all around. They frightened me and I screamed, and then Cegan started demanding explanations.

There was a whole lot of confusion for a moment, with the guards checking under my desk and scanning the corners of the room, and then Mr. Dee and Dad arrived and compounded it. So everyone was yelling at the same time, and I was thinking about crawling under my desk and staying there!

Mr. Dee and Dad calmed everyone down, and Cegan understood, at last, that I wasn't being attacked, and he got quiet. The guards retreated with apologies about having heard a man's voice in the room when I was supposed to be alone. Then, Mr. Dee said he had to leave because he still had some lines to unsnarl, and finally there was only my dad, gazing at me, and me with my heart thumping away madly with no place to look.

I was so ashamed I'd thrust Dad into all this. I felt heavy with guilt. But Dad took a step toward me, and I found myself running into his arms and telling him how sorry I was that I hadn't told him about the marriage. He hugged me tightly and said, "Quiet, Kira. What's done is done. We can only move forward."

The transline was open, and Cegan was still on the line. He'd requested several times in different conversations that he be allowed to talk to my father. I kept telling Cegan that talking with my father was a bad idea, but my husband stubbornly persisted. I knew that their meeting would happen the next day anyway. Perhaps it was better that Dad and Cegan have their first conversation over the transline. At least that way, Dad couldn't punch my husband in the stomach.

"Dad," I said, still dreading their first contact, "Cegan wants to talk with you.

"Please, will you speak with him?"

My dad's face suddenly looked like a stranger's as he burst out, "I have nothing to say to him, Kira. What he's done is wrong."

"Please, Dad. Cegan's waiting on the Teleline. He can hear you right now."

163

My father was shaking his head as if a horde of wasps were after him. I knew how obstinate he could be; I was just like him. "Dad," I said with a sharp burst of anger. "He's my husband, and I love him."

For a moment, Dad glared. Then, his eyes softened. He grabbed me and pulled me back against him, kissing my cheek and smoothing my hair back. When he released me, I studied his eyes, hoping to see that his anger was slightly lessened. I don't think it was, but my mind noted the new wrinkles in his forehead and the way the skin of his face was sagging. Please don't let him get older while I'm gone, I thought. Let him stay forever, the Marlboro Man.

"Dad, please talk with Cegan," I urged again. I could see that he still wanted to refuse, but he sighed heavily and then he nodded his head in resignation.

I smiled my relief and turned to face the speaker. "Cegan, my father is going to have a chat with you now." I was excited and hopeful, but my heart was fluttering about like a caged June bug.

"Mr. Stevens," Cegan began before I'd had the opportunity to show Dad how to work the system. "I am not the son-in-law you would have chosen, but I want you to know that I love Kira, and I will do everything in my power to cherish and protect her."

Dad pressed the button that was supposed to allow Cegan to hear him. "Cegan," he said, his voice so gruff and angry I hardly recognized it, "I don't know who or what you are, but the way you've sweet-talked my daughter out of her common sense is criminal."

"Dad!" I cried out. "Stop it!"

"Kira," he said. "You wanted me to talk to this alien, and now I'm talking to him. You go sit down in that chair over there, and don't interrupt." He was the warden again, scaring all the high school boys away, but I wasn't going to let him do an inquisition on Cegan.

"No, Dad. Cegan is not . . ."

"Kira," my husband said. It was a request. I stopped to listen. "I would like very much to have the opportunity to talk with your father. He has the right to his feelings. Let him speak. I ask you to do this for me."

I couldn't fight both of them. I sighed, but I sat down.

"Kira," Cegan called to me again. "It will truly be more effective if you remain quiet, my love. If you interrupt your father again, it will only make this more difficult."

My dad laughed. "You are a diplomat, Cegan. How is it you understand my daughter so well?"

"Because I love her."

It was the wrong thing to say. My dad launched into a horrible tirade. Cegan would hurt me. Cegan was untrustworthy. Cegan was a dishonorable alien who stole girls for no purpose other than sex.

With that, I bolted up out of my seat and tore the unit out of my father's hands. "I won't listen to this!" I yelled at my dad. "Cegan, I'm sorry. My father knows none of that is true. He's just upset."

"Kira, I am not offended. I understand. He has no reason to trust me and many reasons why he should not. Tell him that he and I will talk later."

I did not bother to repeat Cegan's words. My dad heard them. Whether he listened, I don't know. I walked behind the desk to flip off the Transline-system.

"Kira!" Cegan said. "Wait." My hand froze. "Promise me you will be there tomorrow, my love. Don't let your father's fear or yours stop you. Promise me that."

"I will be there, Cegan. I give you my word."

"Kira, tell your father one more thing."

"What?" I snapped.

"Kira!" Again, I froze. The way Cegan said my name was such a gentle command. I could scarcely argue. "Do not be angry with your father, Kira. Remember what I told you about the needs of a man to protect those he loves?"

I lowered my eyes. I could not look at my father. "Yes, I remember, Cegan." My face was red with embarrassment, but I was listening.

"Do not shut out his love, Kira," my husband told me. "Hold on to every second of the time you have left with him. Promise me."

I sighed, but I gave him my word.

"Good. He and I will talk, Kira, but tell him that we will talk when you are not present."

"Cegan!" What was this? Was he going behind my back?

"Goodbye, my love, until tomorrow."

The line between us went dead. I flipped off my end and shut down the transline. It was a small office, only four white walls, with a single picture of a horse in flight across a jump. I had already emptied my desk taken down my clock, and the poster of Nightmagic was all that was left of me in the room. I unfastened the clips that held it to the wall. I started to roll it up, but my father reached over and took it from me. He placed it down on my desk, and, grasping my shoulders, pulled me close. "Kira, I'm sorry," he said. "Cegan is right. I should not have said that in front of you. I may not like the S.O.B., but there's wisdom in his voice."

Dad hugged me then, and everything was all right again between us. After a moment, he turned, picked up the poster, handed it to me, and lifted up the box in the middle of my desk. With both of us carrying the remnants of my office days, we left Transtel Systems.

Chapter Ten: Definition of an Alien, *Extra-terrestrial*

I had thought that Dad and I would be spending the night at my apartment, but the guards told us that Cegan had specified in his orders that I was not to return home. A "safe house" had been selected for us, and the bureau agents were to drive us to it. I wanted to at least pick up my dress for the next day, but they would not even allow that. Apparently, Cegan had given directions for that as well.

We were hidden in the back of one of their delivery trucks. I think it was for laundry, but it all happened too fast to be sure about anything. There were comfortable seats in the back, with safety belts and even a wet bar, so Dad got his coffee, and I drank a diet soda. We ate some pretzels, too, which reminded us that it was long past noon.

Dad knocked on the back window and said, "Hey, think we can stop for burgers?"

I don't think the agents thought that was very funny. I don't think my Dad really meant it.

Disguised as we were, one would think that our exit from the underground garage would have been easy, but the picketers barred the truck and ranted at the drivers for doing business with Transtel Systems.

"Hey, lady," we heard one of the drivers say, "We're just doing our job. We got nine more pickups today, so just let us get on with it."

The picketers didn't like the driver's answer, and they rocked the truck back and forth a couple of times until the police backed them away from it. My dad and I didn't dare say a word, not even when Dad's coffee jostled all over him. The two guards inside were frozen, their hands on their guns, their eyes fixed on the closed, metal back door.

Apparently, the 'drivers' had been convincing enough, though. With the presence of the police waving us on, the truck was finally given clearance, and we made it through the horde of protestors.

After that, we were no longer thinking of food. Dad tossed his unfinished coffee in the trashcan and said, "I never should have let you leave the farm, young lady."

Everyone smiled, but I knew that Dad wasn't joking.

The safehouse had its own underground garage. We were hustled through it and into an elevator practically before my Dad's legs were uncrinkled. Then, when the elevator door opened again, we were half-pushed, half-dragged into an apartment. Locks were set, and Dad and I were warned that we were not to open the doors. I don't know why they bothered to lecture us because never once was an exit left unguarded.

One of the guards left then, telling us all that he was going to buy pizzas. Dad started smiling again and went over to the couch, turned on the TV, and promptly began to snore. Seeing that, another guard took me upstairs to show me my room. It had a bed with a cream-colored bedspread and drapes of the same color. A vidscreen took up one wall. It was displaying scenes of San Francisco. I recognized the Golden Gate Bridge, although I'd never been there.

I lifted a corner of the drapes to see if there was a view out, but there was only a wall. I turned and met the eyes of the guard. He shrugged. "You'll find a new toothbrush and some other things you might need in the bathroom," he said, pointing to the door on the other side of the room. "In the chest of drawers are clothes, if you wish to change. However, your outfit for the Space Port will be brought to you later. Your . . . husband . . . requested certain items that have not yet been assembled."

"Thank you. Do you have a phone?"

"There will be no calls out, Ms. Stevens."

"Can you let my roommate know that . . .?"

"Ms. Della has already been informed. In fact, she was moved, too. You two are both about the same age, so one of the security chiefs was afraid some dimwit might confuse you and take the wrong girl. Not that I mean we want them to take you . . . ah, you know what I mean."

"Is Cathy angry about it?"

"I wasn't the one who moved her. But, from what I read in her file, I suspect she will look on it as an adventure."

"You have a file on her? Why?"

"Most people don't know this, but there's a file on everyone."

"So you read mine?"

A smile was his answer. I think he would have said more, but the big boss, Joe, had come up behind him. "Is there a problem?"

Sideburns and I both said "no."

"I think, then, that Ms. Stevens will be better off without a lot of chitchats. Go on downstairs."

Joe reminded me of a bulldog one of my friends had owned. It wouldn't let us pet any of my friend's cats. The dog always growled and chased the cats away. We thought at first that it was just jealousy, but it didn't want us to pet or play with it, either. I never could understand a dog like that.

There were jeans in the drawer and a shirt hanging in the closet. Someone had even placed an unopened package of panties and another of socks in the drawer with the jeans. Everything was exactly my size. I showered and changed. My hair was dripping wet, but there was no dryer. It didn't matter much. I usually didn't use one anyway. I toweled my hair dry and ran a comb through it. Whoever had supplied my needs had sure spent a lot of money on good shampoo, cream rinse, and hand cream, plus all the other "essentials" of toiletry.

When I was finished I walked down the stairs, hoping I wasn't being restricted to my room. My timing was great. Terry was just returning with three giant pizzas and two liters of pop. Dad was instantly awake and rose up like his arthritis had miraculously disappeared. He was the first one at the table and was joined by everyone except Joe. Joe stayed at the door, pretending not to watch us eat.

I ate a piece of a new "Super Mammoth." It had everything you could imagine on it: mushrooms, peppers, olives, pineapple, artichoke hearts, spinach, onions, tomatoes, and three or four kinds of meat. It was incredible. Two glasses of soda and I was stuffed! I pushed back from the table and sighed happily. That's when I noticed Joe's eyes on me. I hoped he was only hungry for pizza.

I scooped up a piece of the Super Mammoth and took it to him. I could see that he intended to refuse. The "no" was almost on his lips, but I shoved the paper plate into his hands and backed away. He ate the pizza and came over for a second piece but immediately returned to his post at the door.

I walked over to the bookcase and started looking for a book. The selection was mostly detective novels, the kind that men like with lots of war and politics. But I had nothing else to do, so I kept searching. Good old Dad, having satisfied his hunger, began to converse with the agents. He found out that the guard who had escorted me upstairs was called Dave, and the fourth member was Juan. Juan and Terry were both family men, but Joe and Dave weren't married yet. Dad naturally started concentrating on finding out about Joe and Dave.

I learned that Dave was twenty-six, and Joe was twenty-eight. They had both worked their way through college, a real plus in Dad's opinion. "If it's worth doing, the best way to approach it is by good, old-fashioned hard work. Why, when I was about your age . . ."

I had just pulled out a book and was about to sit down with it when I looked up to see Joe still watching me. I guess I had been mouthing the quotations along with Dad. I'd heard them so many times that it was awfully hard not to. Anyway, Joe must have caught me doing it because he was grinning like a Jack-o-lantern. I blushed, which made it worse because all my friends had always told me that blushing was the grin of flirtation. I sure hoped Joe didn't take it like that.

The book I'd chosen was a good one. Once I started, I was lost in it. I was in Mexico in the heart of an Aztec pyramid and . . .

Dad pried me out of the chair so I could show him where his bedroom was. He could have asked one of the agents, of course, but what that meant was that he wanted me to talk with him. I marked my place with a piece of newspaper that had been lying on the table and led my father up the stairs.

Dad and I talked for a couple of hours, mainly about Cegan and the discussions that my new husband and I had had. Dad did a lot of probing about future plans and then wanted to know about the ship that Cegan was piloting. I couldn't tell Dad a single thing about the ship except that I knew Cegan slept in a bed. Dad tried to drill me for all I knew about Natharan, too, but I really knew next to nothing, and the little I knew, I couldn't tell him. I guess it must have been frustrating for Dad. I was a little weary of saying, "I don't know."

I was thankful when Juan knocked at the door and told us that Terry had returned with dinner. I wasn't very hungry, but it was a relief to be finished with the questioning.

After dinner, which was Chinese food in those little white boxes that have metal lids at the top and which always remind me of the goldfish and turtles I'd carried home from the pet store, Joe cleared the table. He put down a large white piece of paper. Then he started sketching a diagram of SpacePort and explaining what would happen the following day: the plain Autocars, the outfits we'd wear, the way we'd enter, and where we'd stand. Nothing seemed all that unusual until Joe got to the part about how the four of them would get my Dad and me away if anything backfired.

"What do you mean? What could go wrong?" I demanded.

Joe looked me over, just as if he hadn't been doing that ever since we'd arrived at the apartment. "For one thing, you might take one look at the creature, and you . . ."

"You mean my husband?"

"You might take one look at the alien and want out of there quickly. And it is our responsibility to make sure that you are free to do so."

"Good thinking, Joe," said my Dad, giving him a smile that would light up New York.

"I'm not going to change my mind about . . ." I started to say.

"Listen to the man, Kira. He's with the government, and he knows a lot more about this kind of thing than you do."

"He doesn't know Cegan," I said, glaring at my father.

Joe raised his hand for attention. "Ms. Stevens, there are other possibilities that we need you to consider as well. Although we will be screening the area thoroughly, nothing is foolproof. This Natharan captain has suggested that there might be a risk of some kind of bomb in the area."

"Good heavens! You can't take my daughter there," Dad pleaded.

I ignored him. "So what do we do?"

"Good. I wasn't sure what kind of backbone you had."

I leaned forward. "You haven't answered my question, Joe."

"First, the costumes we are providing for you and your father will allow you to blend in with the crowd. Then, when you've made your way to the media, they will surround you, which will offer additional protection since they've all been screened. At that point, you'll be separated, at a distance from all others, with armed guards surrounding you. The four of us may not be able to stand near you. SpacePort has its own security, but we'll wait close by and be specifically on the alert for any signs of detonation devices. That's about all we can do for you."

"That's not enough," my father said.

"Dad, even a tank can be blown up. What more can they do?"

"Should there be the slightest problem, we're also prepared to transport you and your father immediately to another safehouse," Joe continued.

"And Cegan?"

Joe looked uncomfortable with that question. He shifted in his seat and then stared fixedly. "We have reason to believe that your Natharan does not need our assistance. In fact, it is possible that the danger will come from him."

"He's a pacifist! All Natharans are."

Joe's eyes narrowed and grew harder. "You have proof of this, Ms. Stevens? You know beyond a shadow of any doubt that this Natharan has no weapons onboard his ship?"

"I don't understand. How would I have proof? But all the reports and all the documents about Natharan say . . ."

"Exactly what Natharans want us to think, Ms. Stevens."

I backed away from the table abruptly. "I won't listen to this. I know Cegan. You don't. And I trust him more than I trust you, any of you . . . you . . . governmental hypocrites."

"Kira!" Dad called, but I was already running up the stairs and into the room they'd given me. I locked the door, turned off the light, and without putting on the new pajamas still in their plastic wrap, I snuggled under the bedcovers and lay there fighting my tears and doubts.

I heard Dad knocking at the door in a few minutes. I pretended to be asleep, and he went away. I listened as the others bedded down in rooms nearby: the doors and closets opening and closing, the water running, the beds squeaking in protest. One of the men was playing some piano music very softly. It was like the water in our creek at home, gurgling and splashing, leaping over boulders, and racing along with the current.

I woke up when it was still nighttime. For some reason, there was no clock in my room and, of course, no window, yet I knew instinctively that not even the robins would be up yet, foraging for worms. I tiptoed down the stairs, hoping none of the agents would hear my soft tread. I certainly didn't want to talk with them again, not after my tantrum.

Downstairs, it was as black as a cloudy night out on the farm. I closed my eyes for a moment and then opened one. It was a trick that was supposed to allow me to walk into a darkened room. One of the men was sprawled out on the couch, snoring softly. I could just barely make out his form, and the blanket spread across his chest. I knew that my book, unless someone had moved it, was to the side of him, lying on the small table. I crept past him on tippy toes, sliding my feet, not allowing my heel to land against the floor. I was silent as a hunting cat, but a hand grabbed at my wrist and jerked me back and onto the couch.

"What are you up to?" Joe asked, his eyes still closed.

I was too surprised to be angry. "I was just getting my book," I told him meekly.

One forest green eye opened and frowned at me. "Why?" he growled. "Why aren't you sleeping?"

"Please, let go of me," I said.

Instantly, my wrist was free, but I had been pulling back away from him at the same time, and I started to fall. Once more, he grabbed me and yanked me closer.

"Let me go," I said again.

Both of his eyes opened, and he grinned. "We tried that, remember?"

I didn't repeat my words. I dropped my eyes and waited.

"The file says that you're a virgin. Is that true? Did you come down here for a reason, little Kira?"

"Would you like to know how loudly I can scream, Joe?"

He laughed and let me go. I grabbed the book and turned to get out of there.

Joe moved, too, but he only turned on a light. "Sit down," he ordered. Then, as I backed away, he said, "I'm not going to touch you again, Kira. Sit down. I just want to talk to you."

Joe was a lot bigger than me. I could have made a wild dash past him, but I knew he'd stop me. I could have yelled for my father or one of the other agents. I don't know why I didn't, but I sat down on the edge of the chair.

"I'm sorry I scared you, Kira. You took me by surprise. Will you forgive?"

This guy was crazy making. One moment, he attacked, and the next, he apologized. What was left? I nodded.

"You said last night that you didn't trust me. Why?"

"I don't know you," I said before I'd had time to think.

"But you know Cegan?"

Again, I nodded. "If you start on him again, I'm leaving," I warned.

"Suppose I tell you about me. Are you interested?"

"Joe, you've probably been listening to Dad. I don't know what he's told you, but I love Cegan, and I'm a married woman, and anything you tell me is not going to change that one iota."

He flashed his hands in the air, and with a sheepish grin, he said, "All right, I give up. How about a cup of coffee, Ms. Kira? Think that would be a safe proposition?"

"Only if there's no more wrist grabbing."

It was a strange way to spend the "wee hours of the morn," but Joe and I sat down at the table, drank cup after cup of coffee, and talked about things. He was not at all like the bulldog my friend had kept at her farm. Joe was rather a nice guy. I kept trying to think which of my friends I could match him up with. The ones who'd suit him best were married, and neither Frances nor Cathy would work at all.

The others joined us at varying times. First, Terry arrived yawningly, enticed by the smell of coffee. Then, Juan and, later, Dave, each acting like some cartoon character floating in on a stream of coffee vapor. My dad was the last up. He took one look at the coffee pot, which was by then empty, and groaned loudly. I got up to make some more, but Dave waved me back down and took over the job.

Terry, who always seemed to rank the job of food provider, left for a breakfast run. While we waited, we sat around the coffee pot and laughed and chatted as if we were friends. Juan told us about his thirteen-month-old son and how he'd figured out how to push down the shaving cream top and had painted himself with lather.

"Good thing he didn't find the razor," Dad said.

"But he has no hair," Juan said. For some reason, that made us all laugh.

Dave took another sip of coffee and asked innocently enough who'd been the first to come down. Without thinking, I told him that I'd crept down the stairs to get my book. Dave looked over at the book still lying on the table and raised his eyebrows. He shot a glance at Joe and said, "Weren't you sleeping down here?"

My dad, not noticing the sudden strain piped up. "Kira, you read too much. That's an old person's method of travel. You're young. You should be out exploring new outlooks, viewing life with your own eyes, not somebody else's."

Everyone laughed again, and Dad looked around the table, not quite sure of the joke for a moment. When he got it, he added, "I mean exploring this world, Kira, not some planet halfway across the other side of nowhere!"

Terry was back amazing fast, juggling a gallon of orange juice, a large box of doughnuts, and a Styrofoam carton of scrambled eggs with bacon strips on the top. We passed our paper plates and dug in.

"What time is it?" I kept asking what the others told me were "five-minute increments."

"All right," Joe said. "Give her the clothes, Dave. We're not leaving here until 5:00, Kira, but perhaps you'll relax if you're ready."

"When did it get to be *Kira*, Joe?" Dave wanted to know.

"Shut up, Dave," Joe and I said at the same time.

Dad started whistling, "She'll Be Coming Around the Mountain When She Comes." I wanted to tell him to be quiet, too, but of course, I didn't.

Dave handed me the "costume," and I took a peek. "You've got to be kidding!" I exclaimed, holding it out in front of me like it was a dead cat.

 The four men all smiled broadly. Juan said, "Don't glare at us. We just picked it up from the buyers. It's your Natharan who chose it."

I went upstairs without another word, but I wished I could talk to Cegan about his choice of outfits. If that's what he thought I wore, he was in for a real surprise!

I put it on, and my opinion didn't change. The whole thing couldn't have been uglier! The lime green tunic had purple bubbles all over it, and it fell down below my knees! Under it was a long-sleeved lilac tee shirt that picked up the lilac in the bubbles. There were tulip socks, the kind that only reached one's ankles, and they were scalloped all around the top. The socks were also in lilac and, I suppose, matched the lime-green-and-purple marbled tennis shoes.

Oh, I'm not saying it wasn't in style. It was probably the hottest attire for the season, but I hated it. I'd always felt that if everyone was wearing blue, it was a great time to wear green. I hated being a fashion clone.

I didn't bother fixing my hair; I'd already been told I'd be wearing a wig. I shuddered to think what that would look like.

The men, except for Dad, whose sole concession to the masquerade had been to wear a less farm-looking shirt, were all wearing varying colors of jumpsuits. To me, they looked ridiculous. Juan had a spotted scarf around his neck, which made him fashionably the most "with-it." They were all wearing sharp-edge wigs, which gave them the appearance of someone who'd messed with a loose electric wire.

Dave put my wig on me and adjusted it for me. It was cotton candy pink and jutted out to the side. I thought that was bad enough until Juan added the final touch. A scarlet rose tattoo that scanned from my right cheek clear across my forehead. I was headed to the mirror to take a look when Joe wickedly called out, "We're going to be late; let's go!"

I ran to the downstairs bathroom anyway and screeched when I saw how dreadful I looked.

"You sure you want to go, Kira?" Dad asked.

Dumb question! I was still the first at the door and tapping my foot restlessly when Dave said he'd left the car keys upstairs.

Chapter Eleven: Definition of Alien, *Hostile*

When we finally got to SpacePort, we were still almost an hour early. Even so, the whole area was lit up like the opening of a new department store. Beacon lights were flashing blues and reds. Floodlights were scanning, searching for dark corners. The place was filled with reporters, TV broadcasters, the curious, the angry, and people who just wanted to be there because it was something different, an event not to be missed.

The noise level, from the exuberant greetings of friends meeting friends, the conversations, the yelling and the screaming of picketers who were arguing back and forth, and the media, readying of equipment and interviewing people for their on-the-street opinions, was an assault on my courage. I didn't want to go anywhere near that mob, to be part of all that. But I had to.

Dave and Terry went on ahead, and my father and I followed. Joe and Juan brought up the rear. When Dad and I needed to walk into the midst of the crowd, pressing our way forward, it felt like we were alone. I knew Dad was as scared as I was, but he never let me know it. His hand held mine firmly, and although he let me take the lead, he was there beside me. A tree to lean on, wasn't that what Cegan had called him?

I tried to play the part of a brass young "trend model." Joe had assured me I looked the part, but I didn't feel like it. Several people, glancing askance at my father, didn't believe it either. They barred our way.

"Hey, youngster, I'm meetin' someone. Pass me by," I said, pointing further ahead. Grudgingly, they let us push on through. I was impressed with the jargon that Joe and his team had ferreted out. Obviously, it was very "mode."

My face had been splashed on TV screens and in every newspaper, but no one recognized me. No one really looked at my face at all, or I guess if they did, all they saw was the rose tattoo and my pink hair. Perhaps everyone figured that Cegan's bride would arrive inside a police brigade or a fancy pilotcar.

My dad and I just continued edging forward. We were at the front of the crowd, almost to the media line, before one of the reporters yelled out, "Hey, I think that's her! I think that's Kira Stevens, the one the alien married!"

Our four guards packed in around Dad and me then, and they pulled us into the media area. The police held the others back, and we quickly moved forward. The same man, the one who'd called out, stuck a microphone under my chin and demanded that I tell the viewers why I'd married an alien.

The reporter wore a dark blue pin-striped suit with an orange tie. I kept staring at his tie, wondering what I was doing in front of all those cameras with their little lights the same orange as the man's tie, flashing and twirling, flashing and twirling.

"Move back," Joe ordered them. "Can't you see that you're scaring her to death?"

Dad was on one side of me, and Joe was on the other. I shouldn't be panicking. Cegan would be landing any moment. Could he see the broadcast? I took a deep breath.

"I married Cegan because I love him," I said, watching the orange light revolve around and around.

"Kira Stevens," another man began. "Tell us about the alien you've married."

I started to speak, to tell the man that Cegan was a Natharan, but I had just seen Frances. She was standing only a couple of feet away, talking and posing the way she always did, thrusting out her chest. I smiled to see her flirting with the cameras as skillfully as she flirted with men.

She had on her shiny gold metallic sheath dress with the open panels on the sides, the one she'd modeled for the cover of Time. Frances' hand swept back her long black hair. She gathered it up to the side, raked it with her fingers, and then tossed it back behind her. If I'd done that, my hair would have been a mess. On Frances, the gesture worked. She was gorgeous.

Frances must have felt me watching her. She looked over to the side. Her eyes rounded. Then, she waved and came rushing over, a crowd of reporters in her wake. She kissed both of my cheeks.

"You're not angry with me, are you?" she whispered into my ear.

I laughed. "Cegan said all this madness was inevitable, Frances. I just wish I'd told my father before it blew open."

Frances shot a glance at my dad. I introduced them.

"You never told me how handsome he is," Frances said, giving Dad one of her especially flirtatious smiles.

Dad's eyebrow suddenly dropped to half-mast. "Nice to meet you," he told her formally and coldly.

Frances shrugged and smiled at me, "It's been a wild ride, Kira. Thanks for being such a good sport about it." She glanced out into the group of reporters surrounding us. Raising her voice to carry, she asked, "Are you scared, Kira? You know, about seeing Cegan for the first time."

I don't know if Frances was really curious or had been bribed to ask me that question. I do know that when I struggled to answer, Frances was no longer beside me, and what seemed like a hundred microphones were suddenly thrust into my face. "Yes, of course, I'm frightened by all of this," I said. Dad squeezed my hand, and I smiled, grateful for his presence.

"What will be your first words to your husband?" asked a smiling blonde in a tight-fitting green-and-orange Dinacut dress. Her dress was so short the matching peek-a-boo panties showed even when she wasn't raising her arms up in the air.

"I don't know. Hello?"

I saw the flash of disappointment in her eyes. Couldn't I have said something original, something sharp, like Frances would have said?

"Where will you spend your honeymoon?" asked a man about my father's age.

"I don't know," I told him, shrugging. I was trying not to think about honeymoons.

"Your friend, Frances, says you have no idea what your husband looks like. Is that true, Ms. Stevens?"

I had already noticed that reporter: six feet tall, with football shoulders, a smile that devastated.

"No. I mean, yes, it's true."

"What do you think he looks like?" the man continued to probe.

Why had we come to SpacePort so early? All I wanted was to be alone . . . and to think. A camera flash bolted me out of my thoughts. My eyes were blinded. I shut them.

"You are very beautiful, Ms. Stevens. Does the alien know that?"

I opened my eyes to stare into the big browns of the reporter. His teeth were toothpaste commercial white. His eyes were admiring. I blushed and dropped my gaze.

Frances chose that moment to push back into the front. Maybe Mr. Brown Eyes was her newest flame. She wedged herself into his sight. "Kira's never seen her husband, and he's never seen her. Didn't you hear that already?"

Mr. Brown Eyes scanned Frances' body. It only took a moment. Then his eyes were once more staring into mine. "Ms. Stevens, I would imagine that the space captain, Thenus Sachem, told the alien about your appearance. Do you think an alien can truly appreciate your beauty as much as a human male would?"

He was embarrassing me. I had no idea how to answer.

"Enough," my father interrupted. "You will leave my daughter alone. Come on, Kira, let's go."

Juan pushed forward. Joe held onto my other elbow.

"Mr. Stevens!" "Mr. Stevens!" "Mr. Stevens!" The reporters suddenly went wild, trying to catch my father's attention. Dad ignored them. Perhaps we would have been allowed to escape the media, after all, since I hadn't been an interesting person to interview, but the handsome one, the one with the huge brown eyes, stepped in front of us. Once more, I felt those eyes studying me, but he didn't ask me anything. He turned to my father. "Mr. Stevens, what do you think about your daughter marrying an alien?"

Dad glowered at the guy. For a moment, I thought my father would ignore the question and push on past, but then he paused. I could almost see the light bulb turning on. "What's your name?" my dad asked the reporter.

Terry and Dave were catching up. They passed us and circled to the left.

"John Gether."

"You a married man? How many years have you been with your paper? You can't be more than what, twenty-five?"

"Dad!" I said angrily, knowing where this was going. Joe, on my right, laughed softly. I tried to push forward, but my father had too strong a hold on my elbow.

Once more, the reporter's incredible smile flashed. It had begun to irritate me, especially when he kept trying to catch my eye with it.

"No, I'm not married. I've been with the Interglobal four years, and I'm twenty-four, Mr. Stevens."

"I see," said my Dad, ignoring all the other reporters. "Well, Mr. Gether, my daughter is an adult, so there isn't much I can do about all this, but I will tell you, and you can print this, Mr. Gether, I love my daughter, and whatever she does, that love is the one thing that will never change. You understand, Mr. Gether?"

"Yes, Mr. Stevens. I understand. But I think you'll agree with me; it sure seems a waste for someone like your daughter to be marrying a freakin' alien."

I raised my eyes to Mr. Gether. I was sure mine were shooting sparks. I forgot about the crowds and the reporters and all the picketers yelling at me. "Mr. Gether," I began . . .

"Call me John, please?"

"Mr. Gether, I am here to meet my husband, whom I love very much. I love him because of who he is, because of the way he speaks, and because of his thoughts and beliefs. You wouldn't understand that, would you? But how Cegan looks is not important. If you think that is a waste, that is your problem. When was the last time you had a philosophical discussion?"

Joe began to chuckle. The reporter shot a quick glance at him and then smiled wider. "May I quote you, Ms. Stevens?"

"Yes, if you'll leave me alone," I snapped.

"Of course," he said, still grinning impudently.

I stared up into the empty sky, wishing Cegan's ship would hurry.

"Ms. Stevens," Mr. Gether called back over his shoulder as we pressed on. "Anytime you'd like to have that philosophical discussion, I'd be happy to oblige."

Beside me, my father chuckled, and Joe joined in.

I glared at both of them. "Not a word, Dad. Don't even start, and Joe, I thought you were supposed to be guarding me, not aiding and abetting my father in his matchmaking."

"You're right, Kira. Let's move you over to that isolation place we talked about. After all, we wouldn't want any other reporters bothering you with their big-toothed grins!"

A small black ship shot out of the sky and began dropping down into the berther. I froze to watch, fascinated by the sight. I was aware that Juan and Terry were now behind me, and Dave had staked out Dad's other side. (And, of course, I was aware of Joe, who was still grinning down at me and holding onto my elbow like I was a lifebuoy in the middle of the ocean.)

As the little ship came closer, it took on the appearance of a badly wrinkled potato. I knew it then from sketches I'd seen at Transtel Systems. It was a Cedtarant ship. I wondered if the captain I'd talked to at Transtel Systems was on board. That had been such a strange conversation. I remembered how Cegan had said that Cedtarants liked Terrans. I sure hoped that they still felt that way after this visit.

The six of us continued to pause our forward movement as the port's berthing nets enwrapped the little ship and settled it down into its resting position. The smell of burning ozone filled the air. The sound of its landing caught up with the ship and thundered the concrete beneath our feet. My feet vibrated. My legs were shaking. The tremors from the ship and my nervousness combined. Body quake.

"Don't be afraid. It isn't the Natharan," Joe shouted in my ear.

"Of course not! That's a Cedtarant ship," I said.

Cedtarants were fairly common at SpacePort. Many attended the Academy. I'd seen them before from a distance, but never up this close. I watched as seven of them climbed out of their ship. Their long, graceful antennae hung at their sides like disappointed rabbits, and their elongated, pink-skinned bodies made them seem like they flowed down the ramp.

My father sputtered. "They have antennas, Kira! Antennas like an insect!"

"Sh!" I hushed him quickly. "They're very nice, and they like Terrans. Cegan told me so."

"What — for breakfast?" Dad continued.

Three officials dressed in the black and red of the SpacePort uniform were meeting the Cedtarants. The officials waited for the aliens to walk towards them and then exchanged ceremonial greetings. They all started walking towards one of the large black pilotcars that Space Port maintained for its private business. But then they halted for a moment, and I saw the Cedtarants first looking over in my direction and then at the huge crowd assembled behind the police line.

A minute passed; Dad was urging us to "get where we were supposed to be," but something about the attitude of the Cedtarants and the way they kept looking at us made me think that we shouldn't move away yet.

I was correct. One of the black and reds turned away from the group and walked toward us. The SpacePort official, a very dark African American with broad shoulders and gorgeous mahogany eyes, continued walking until he stood directly in front of me. "You are the former Kira Stevens," he demanded.

"Yes."

"Come with me."

"Why?"

The official shrugged, and I shot a nervous glance at Dad. "I'll come, too," my father said. He threw his arm around my shoulder, and we set off to follow behind the SpacePort official.

My protection group tagged along, too, and the official was either not aware of that fact or chose to ignore it. In fact, he made no comment to any of us until we'd walked to within about ten feet of the aliens. Then he stopped and said, "The rest of you will wait here. Only Ms. Stevens may go closer."

"Wait a minute," Joe argued. "Our job is to see that she's safe. We can't do that if you take off with her and lead her into what looks to me to be a dangerous situation."

"May I see your I.D.?"

Joe pulled a metal disk out of his chest pocket and handed it to the black and red.

The official scanned it with some kind of handheld device that he kept in his chest pocket. "You do not have clearance to approach the Cedtarants. I assume that is true of the rest of you?"

Juan, Terry, and Dave all handed over their I.D.'s. The official waved his I.D. checker over theirs, too, and then shook his head. "And you, sir?" he said to my father.

"I don't even have what they have," Dad said.

"Only the girl goes," the official repeated.

"She doesn't have clearance for this either, I bet," Joe said.

The official smiled nastily. "Of course, she does. She's a Natharan."

Then, the official looked down at me, and he smiled a very different smile. This one was warm and friendly. "Are you ready?" he asked. "Do not fear the Cedtarants. They will not hurt you in spite of what these agents think."

"Kira, they can't make you go, can they?" Dad asked.

I kissed his cheek and said, "It's all right, Dad. I'll be right back."

I accompanied the official, and as we walked towards the waiting group, the man said, "You must be very polite, young lady, and remember that even though you're a Natharan, you're still a representative of Earth. I'm sure you know that we wish to keep the Cedtarants as allies."

While he was lecturing me about protocol, my mind barely heard him. I was only wondering why the Cedtarants wanted to see me. Had

I done something wrong? Did they know Cegan? What did they want with me?

The distance to the aliens was not far, but my legs felt like gelatine. Not only was I the only amusement of thousands of people who were watching, and not only was this probably being taped by twenty or so cameras, but I was frankly scared stiff because, although I'd talked to lots of aliens over the transystem, I'd never actually been close to a single one of them.

The group of officials and Cedtarants turned to face me. They were staring. The thick, pointy antennae of the aliens were slightly lifted, about midway from where they normally perched. Did that mean something? Were they angry?

They smelled like stale breadcrumbs. My stomach churned. I stopped a foot away. I did not know the correct proximity distance for Cedtarants. Was I at an equal distance from the officials, or were they closer?

One of the pink guys stepped a clawed pace closer toward me. He wore no shoes, and his toenails clicked against the cement.

"You are the wife of the Natharan, Cegan Caste Five?" the Cedtarant asked me, holding his hands up for me to touch his fingertips.

I had to stretch upwards on tiptoes. His hands were not so far up there, but the fingers had a twelve-inch reach. The alien saw my problem and lowered his hand. For the five seconds required, my fingertips pressed against his. His fingers were icy cold. I suppressed my shudder and dropped my hands. "Yes. I am Cegan's wife," I whispered, looking down at the ground.

Cegan had never mentioned anything about Caste Five. Where did that come from? Cegan had said he didn't have a last name. I would have questioned the Cedtarant about it if I'd been feeling better, but I suddenly felt ill. There was something about the way the Cedtarant was moving its mouth that made me feel worse.

The pink guy didn't seem to notice. "It is good. This co-mingling. We Cedtarants approve. We like you, Terrans. We like Natharans, too. Felicitation on your joining."

A hundred questions were on my lips, but I didn't ask them. I was concentrating too hard on not throwing up. "Thank you," I said.

The Cedtarant turned and walked back to his group. I went the other way. When I reached my dad, he enclosed me in his strong, farmer's arms. We stood there a moment, and nobody said anything. I took several gulps of fresh air.

The black-and-red uniform came up behind me and touched my shoulder. "You did well, Wife of Cegan, Caste Five. The Cedtarants often make Terrans ill. Many of us vomit from their proximity."

"Why?"

The man just shrugged. He spoke into a hand plant, a small microphone melded into his skin. "Why are there no SpacePort officials here to guard the wife of the Natharan? Are you fools? I will give you one minute to have five guards here. Out."

The official's eyes kept fanning the crowd and the area around us. He indicated with a head thrust to the right that we should continue to our designated place. We were almost there when the five guards arrived at a military run.

"I.D.," the black-and-red commanded of the newcomers.

He checked each one of theirs thoroughly and then turned back to me. "Wife of Cegan, Caste Five, it has been a privilege to serve you. I must return to my post. Captain Brish will take over now."

A man with white-blond hair stepped forward and saluted. With his broad chest and towering manner, he looked like a Viking, strangely clothed in the black and red uniform of a port official.

 "Thank you," I said, turning to the official who'd escorted me to the Cedtarants. He bowed, and his eyes scanned over the agents who stood beside us.

"Captain Brish, you will allow these men to stay with Ms. Stevens," he ordered. "They have provided her with the only protection she's been given so far at SpacePort. Without them, I shudder to think what might have happened."

"Yes, sir."

Then he was gone, walking back towards the Cedtarants, who were waiting in the pilotcar. From our new spot, we watched as the official rejoined his party.

When the pilotcar lifted and was no longer in sight, I thought the noise and all the people would kind of settle down, but the Cedtarants had somehow energized the picketers. They grew rowdier. Their protests carried above all the other noises. "Alien-lover, alien bride. Terran traitor, where's your pride?"

The chant became louder and louder. A couple of the protesters even broke through the crowd, banging their placards down on the innocent heads of the police as they surged forward towards us. "Alien-lover, Alien bride, Terran traitor, where's your pride?"

The new guards pulled stunners out of the holsters on their boots and raised them pointedly at the chanters. It froze the forward momentum, but it didn't silence the group. A fresh wave of policemen came rushing over. They gathered the disruptive marchers and led them away. The marchers changed their chant. "Alien bride, where's your pride? Alien bride, where's your pride." And then, as they were being led away, most of them struggling against the cop cuffs and restrictive holds, their volume increased. "No pride, alien bride. No pride, alien bride. No pride . . ."

Within the main body of the crowd, a restlessness was growing. The people were more strident. Police in riot squad uniforms brought in horses and dogs. An increasing number of red-and-black SpacePort officials moved in to stand guard at the line, holding back the crowd.

I couldn't understand all of this. I was only one person, a girl from a farm in rural New York. What was fueling all this anger?

Dad reached over and threw his arm around my shoulders again. He pulled me towards him and kissed my cheek. It was the only sanity in all the confusion.

Already, a new group of protestors was fermenting. This one had a loudspeaker. "There was Adam, and there was Eve, and their union was blessed. God did not say, 'Go forth and mate with other species.' He did not tell Adam and Eve to engage in carnality with beings unlike them. God said, 'Go forth and be fruitful with each other.' Kira Stevens, do you think that God will forgive you if you fornicate with alien beasts? Will God forgive you, Kira Stevens, if you whore among the stars? What are the wages of sin, Kira? What are the wages of sin. . .?"

"I can't take this, Dad. I can't . . ."

Dad shifted me around and pulled me closer. "I love you, Kira," he said. "No matter what happens here. I love you."

I darted him a kiss on the cheek, and then I lay my head on his steady, beating heart. Was I wrong for doing what I was doing? Would God understand? I closed my eyes and prayed. I asked God to help me, and then I listened. For a long time, I tried not to think about the sermon that was still going on, or what the chanters were singing, or even the Cedtarants whose mere proximity had frightened me so badly that I'd felt physically sick.

My mind drifted, and I could almost hear Cegan. *The essence of God is found in every civilization, Kira. The one you harbor in your soul melds well with the essence that is within me. There is no conflict of Gods between us.*

I sighed and let my mind drift further. *Trust your soul to recognize the Truth*; I knew Cegan would tell me again. But what if Natharans were like Cedtarants? What if the sight of Cegan made me feel sick?

"Please, God, please help me to recognize the soul of Cegan when I look at his face for the first time. Please don't make me see only his alienness. Please, God," I whispered inside my head.

"Kira, are you all right?" my father was asking.

I moved back slightly so I could look up at him. "Yes, Dad. I'm OK. It was a moment of panic."

"Good, because you're about to have a visitor," my father told me, and my eyes focused on the middle-aged female who was rapidly moving towards us. She was a tall, healthy-looking woman, dressed almost militarily, in a slim, dark, navy suit. She strode with a walk faster than an Olympic sprinter. But she slowed and then stopped to show Captain Brish something that was in her hand. He scanned it with a metal shielder and then nodded that she could advance toward us.

"Hello, Ms. Stevens," she greeted me.

I nodded but said nothing.

"I am from the United Liberties Organization. I have come here to assure you that you will always be protected under our American laws, no matter how the Natharans treat women."

I was listening to her speech, but it was difficult not to laugh. Her voice came from a long, tubular-looking nose. The woman wasn't malformed exactly, but her nose was far too prominent for her face. The fact that it carried all her words made it difficult to concentrate on anything else. My eyes dropped to the pin she wore on her suit. The three scales of justice meant that she was a member of the Trinational conference. I'd seen parts of that conference in the videocams.

"You may call on the U.L.O. for help should you ever have the slightest need. And, if that alien husband of yours ever lays a hand on you, we will go to bat for you. We protect our own, no matter where they live, Ms. Stevens."

"Thank you," I said, wondering how an agency light years away would help me if I were really in trouble. And what could the United Liberties Organization do to help me if they weren't allowed to land on Natharan?

"Were you really at the Trinational conference?" I asked her when she seemed finished with her address.

Her eyes were black, not like obsidian, but more the color of old asphalt, with shades of brown from the layers of dirt that sifted down. She peered at me, examining me.

"Are you a believer of the union?" she trumpeted.

My father was standing beside me. He shifted. I wondered if his legs were hurting him.

"No," I answered her. "I will always be an American. The Trinational would take that away from us."

Dad cleared his throat. I thought he might speak, too, but he only reached out and patted my arm.

"I see," said the woman coldly. She turned away from us and made her way through the guards back to wherever she'd come from.

"Guess I didn't make her very happy," I said.

"You don't have to say everything you're thinking, Kira," Dad berated me.

"I like Kira's attitude," Joe piped in.

"I think she's right," Terry and Juan defended me.

I smiled at them and turned to watch the woman as she retreated. A short, rather pudgy man was walking toward her. The woman stopped when she came even with him, shook hands, chatted with him a moment, and then moved on.

A moment later, the blue-suited man, weaving his way among our guards and flashing his credentials at each of them, came closer. He was introduced by the Viking port official as the American Ambassador of the Trinations. I suspected that Ambassador Dwibe was probably about nine or ten years younger than Dad, but he didn't have my Dad's physique. He was fat and breathing heavily from the short walk. Perspiration dripped from his forehead. He pulled out a black handkerchief and wiped at the sweat accumulation.

James Dwibe, he told us his name was, was wearing dark-green vision goggles, the kind that lets you see further in the distance than usual. He didn't take off the goggles as he reached out and shook first Dad's hand and then mine. "And you men, are you friends of Ms. Stevens?" he asked, looking at the agents.

I didn't say anything. They were kind of friends by now, but the men hadn't started out that way.

"We are here for the protection of Ms. Stevens," Joe informed him.

I swear that the ambassador's nose lifted up about three centimeters. Then, without another word to Joe, Mr. Dwibe turned his back on him.

Just like the U.L.O. lady, Mr. Dwibe gave me a card with his name and phone number and then gave me a lecture about being protected by American law, no matter where I lived. "Do not be afraid to call on us," he said, taking rasping breaths between almost every word.

"We will one day have embassies all over the universe. Already, we have them on Venus, Mars, and several moons, and there is talk about adding one to our outpost on Pluto, too." He snorted a laugh, inhaled sharply a couple of times, and said, "In the future, I bet we'll even have one on Natharan."

I didn't point out to Mr. Dwibe that I probably wouldn't be visiting any Terran outposts and that I doubted that Natharan wanted an American embassy. But, although I really wanted to discuss the Trinational issue with him because I couldn't understand how he thought he could represent the U.S. and two other countries when that seemed to me to be such an obvious conflict of interest, I remembered what my father had said about not having to say everything I was thinking.

And, besides, the ambassador seemed to be in a great hurry, fidgeting and turning about restlessly as if he had to go to the bathroom urgently or he couldn't wait to get out of there.

I put the U.L.O. card into my purse, with the one that the woman had given me (I supposed the cards would be interesting souvenirs), and thanked him for coming over to see me. Mr. Dwibe waddled away with a quick goodbye and a great deal of huffing and panting.

During the exchange with the ambassador, a couple of the guards had brought Dad and me chairs. The chairs were the kind that you place on the ground, then you push a small button, and they rise up like magic from some inner inflation device. Dad collapsed on his chair immediately, and I felt terribly guilty that I hadn't realized how much he was hurting from all the standing around.

I stood next to my chair and called out to the SpacePort officials. "Could you please bring four more of those chairs for my friends?" I was still bothered by the ambassador's snub of the agents. I hoped that their feelings hadn't been hurt, and besides, I knew that they must be just as tired as I was.

Joe moved closer, put his hand on my shoulder, and pushed downwards. "Sit down, Kira. We're not here for a tea party, silly."

I moved over and deposited my posterior into the chair. When I looked up, everyone, including Dad, was grinning at me. Dad leaned over and whispered into my ear. "I think you made a conquest with Joe. A bureau agent wouldn't be such a bad husband, now would it?"

"Stop it, Dad," I snapped and tried to ignore the sudden heat in my face.

The police line was still holding. The policemen were dressed in their shock padding and were armed with stun pistols. The crowd was respectful of that, but their numbers were growing larger. The noise was tumultuous, with the steady chanting of the protestors and the yelling of so many excited and excitable people.

I could see that the media, in front and over to the side, had become a greater force, also. Flashes were still going off periodically, focused in my direction, reminding me that, although I was away from the crush of journalists, I was still under their eye and being recorded. Several times, as I watched, a cameraman attempted to break out of his restricted area and come closer.

I wondered how many pictures of me they could possibly want. I cringed when I remembered my rose tattoo, pink wig, and ridiculous lime-green jumper.

I tilted Dad's wrist and shot a glance at his watch. The minute hand was clinging, not moving at all. I almost wanted more excitement, more picketers, more ambassadors, more aliens desiring to talk, anything to speed up the time. Unbelievably, there were still fifteen minutes to go.

My eyes searched the sky. It was a gray day, slightly cloudy, but with the hint that perhaps the sun would break through. Would I be able to see the ship when it breached the outer atmosphere, or would the cloud cover prevent us from noticing its arrival?

What would I say to Cegan? What would we do when we first set eyes on each other? Why did our first meeting have to be so public? Why did Cegan and I have to meet with cameras flashing and spectators everywhere? I wished I could scream over a loudspeaker, "Everyone go home. This is private."

Chapter Twelve: Definition of Alien, *Scary?*

An abrupt buzz of the SpacePort alarm sounded. A ship was coming in. Was it Cegan's? The time, by my father's watch, was 5:55. I scanned the skies. There was only the gray of formless clouds. No ship was in sight. The crowd struggled against the police line. A scream pierced the air. "There it is! There it comes!"

You could see it then. A metal disk, shiny and slightly red, was winking in and out. Surely, it was just an airplane. The blinking light was just the warning light on its tail.

But then it grew bigger and still bigger. It was coming down fast. It wasn't an airplane. It wasn't anything like the ships of the Baskantes, Qweldons, or Cedtarants. This ship was the size of my old town library!

The SpacePort's warning buzz droned louder. I clapped my hands over my ears. "Stop it," I wanted to shout, but the noise went on and on. There hadn't been more than one tell-tell beep for the Cedtarant's ship. Why did the clamor persist? Why didn't someone turn it off?

The giant elliptical ship was losing most of its sheen. It was redder, fire-red. Was that OK? Was it supposed to look like it was burning? Was it Cegan's ship?

The SpacePort officials seemed to think so. They were motioning us to get up and go with them. Joe gave me a hand and pulled. I turned to help Dad, but the others had already seen him.

"It's not too late to leave, Kira," Joe told me, still holding on to my elbow as he had when we'd first arrived.

"I think that's my husband," I told him, not taking my eyes off the massive ship descending now at a slower rate.

"At any time, Kira. You give the word, and we'll pull off your wig and the tattoo and slip you into the crowd without them being any the wiser."

I shot a glance at Joe. He was such a nice man, but how could he possibly think I'd desert Cegan now? I shook my head. "I won't leave."

"All right. The others and I will stay at your side, Kira. We'll try to protect you from the Natharan, but we don't know anything about his technology. It could be too late once this Cegan sees you. It would be safer, Kira, for you to leave before . . ."

I pulled away from him. "You don't understand! I have to see Cegan. I want to see him. He's my husband."

"Kira, listen to me," Joe said, pulling on my elbow again. "You're not doing this for publicity. I realize that now. You're a good kid . . ."

"I'm not a kid!" I said, whirling around to face him. "Let go of me."

"I'm sorry, Kira. I know you're not. You're a woman, one I'd like to see a lot more of . . ."

"Stop it! Leave me alone!"

Joe dropped my elbow as if I'd slapped him and moved away. I had only an instant of guilt, but he was a distraction I didn't need or want, and I didn't have time to worry about his feelings. Cegan was landing!

We had walked as close to the ship's berth as was safe. Some of the SpacePort officials were already working, roping off a section for the ship's estimated circumference. It must have been difficult to calculate where to place their warning ribbons because the ship was hovering about three hundred feet up, still aligning itself to the berthing web. Was it Cegan's ship?

It must be, yet none of us knew that for certain. Its appearance certainly didn't match any of the ships I'd seen on file. This one was distinctively different in shape and color from any of those displayed in the Transtel Systems downstairs gallery, and it was so much bigger than I had imagined any ship to be. I guess I'd expected a Natharan ship to be the same size as a Cedtarant's. This ship was a rodeo arena, an ocean liner, or a football stadium.

Once more, the immense metal egg proceeded to lower. It was no longer reddened by its struggle with gravity; now it was a dull, blackened iron-looking metal, with circles or ringlets of what looked like copper scrolling about its rim. Those circlets blinked on and off. At times, they shone so brightly that it almost hurt our eyes to look at them.

As SpacePort's magnetic web attempted to enfold the huge ship's bulk, accepting more and more of the weight, a dull, low, moaning groan of protest began to vibrate through our feet and ears. It sounded like the web was buckling under the enormous weight. I wondered if we should back up.

My father suddenly clutched at my hand. He leaned over and whispered into my ear, "There's no mistake that cannot be corrected, Kira. Remember that."

He had told me that so many times growing up. I smiled up at him. I didn't know if he'd done it on purpose or not, but Dad had given me back the stubbornness my bravery needed. It was that smile, with my shoulders flung back, my head held erect as if flaunting my rebellion at Dad's all-too-fatherly words, that some far-off camera with a translinephoto captured. It is Cegan's favorite picture. He calls it "Independence."

But I wasn't thinking of posing or of cameras flashing. The spaceship was so close now, not more than twenty feet. It had started emitting hand-like padded platforms that were extending out and down. They touched the ground, absorbing most of the weight of the ship, and the Earth-bound magnetic web stopped its groaning.

At the same second, we all stepped backwards, assaulted by the terrible ferocity of the heat contained in the dull surface of the ship. The smell of the metal began to permeate the air around us. It wasn't all that unpleasant, but it caused several of us to cover our noses. You could tell the surface of the ship was cooling. This close, it was like having a heater blasting warmth in your face. And, as if we hadn't known, faint cracking sounds alerted us to its changing temperatures.

The great, mammoth egg was now fully on the ground. The circlets were no longer flashing. They had dulled to match the rest of the ship's surface. I don't know what I expected, but shouldn't a voice ring out? "Attention, Earthlings, I am Cegan, the Natharan."

But there was no announcement; only a faint hum persisted and the occasional cracklings from the stress of the cooling metal.

My heart was pounding. I felt dizzy and slightly nauseated, almost like I'd felt when I visited the Cedtarant. My throat ached, and I could barely swallow. Joe reached out. I pushed him away. Dad squeezed my hand.

And then a door was sliding open. I could see a kind of ramp descending. It looked like white lava flowing downwards. My legs began to tremble.

The newspaper reporters and the cameramen stampeded forward, and the police and SpacePort officials lost all control. The purple ribbons that the SpacePort officials had mounted about the huge egg were broken and tossed aside, and the media pushed in closer around Cegan's ship. Only my four agents from the Bureau and the SpacePort officials surrounding me protected Dad and me from being crushed in their charge.

I was desperate to catch a glimpse of a Natharan, but I couldn't see a thing. I bit my tongue to keep from yelling out my frustration. I measured the seconds that passed by the beating of my speeding heart.

Yet, not more than a minute could it have been before the police forced the media back, and the cameras were swinging once again to my face.

And then, for the first time, I saw a Natharan. As if someone had suddenly rammed his fist into my middle, all the breath in me exhaled.

To Continue on, read:

Book 2 of The Trust Series

You Can Trust Some Aliens